PROLOGUE

'Hope is the life we think we lost.'

Connie

THE MIST APPEARED to be crawling towards me. I didn't move, refusing to let it push me away. I'd been pushed away too many times and I wouldn't allow anyone or anything to do it again.

My heart ached as I stood under the cover of the trees, their heavily laden branches providing a secluded hideaway as I watched the small congregation gather by the graveside. A couple of people opened umbrellas when the rain began to fall heavier, immediately dampening down the curling fog.

I recognised most of them. I was surprised Tammy had come; she'd always bullied Mae at school. And Bonnie, another two-faced bitch me and my sister had avoided like the plague.

I swiped at the tears that flooded down my cheeks. A part of me had gone, evaporated from inside me. My soul felt incomplete, my heart had split down the middle.

I couldn't decipher what the vicar was saying from so far away but I didn't need his words. They wouldn't comfort me nor would they take away the ache or the guilt. Bonnie wailed when the vicar threw a lump of soil on top of Mae. What the fuck? Dramatic skank.

My eyes widened when a tall dark-haired man stepped out from behind a woman with a large umbrella. I hadn't noticed him before, and from the sheer size of him I wondered why. His long black coat was drenched, his dark brown hair slicked across his forehead as streams of rain ran down his face. I could see the drops dripping from his long eyelashes even from the distance between us.

He stood by the edge of the hole, looking down into it with a severe frown. He looked angry; angry at Mae for dying possibly. I understood because I felt it too. The rage that had engulfed me when one of my contacts notified me of her death had been the most unreal feeling I had ever felt, even greater than the grief of losing my parents… or rather my mother.

I cocked my head in puzzlement when he dropped a single deep red rose onto her coffin. His fists clenched before he brought one up to his lips and kissed it then tossed something else into the grave.

Loud sobs filtered across the cemetery, the driving rain doing nothing to stop the weeping as people wandered off.

Waiting until everyone had left, I trudged across the muddy ground and stopped beside my sister's final resting place.

"Hey," I whispered as I brought my gaze down to the wooden box that held Mae. A deep tightening in my chest brought on a gasp of pain and I closed my eyes for a moment. The rain beat down on me, punishing me for the sins I had committed against my own flesh and blood. "I'm so sorry, Mae."

The silence tore at me until the pain became too much and I stepped back to leave. A splash of white from the coffin caught my attention. It was obviously what the tall guy had thrown in. I squinted, trying to focus on what it was but I couldn't make it out.

Pulling my phone from my inside pocket, I quickly snapped a shot of the object. Opening up the camera album, I swiped at the screen as the rain beaded, distorting the image before I zoomed in

THE SALVATION OF
DANIEL

Book 2 in
The Blue Butterfly Series

D H SIDEBOTTOM

and stared in shock.

I stumbled backwards, losing my footing, my heart thudding loudly in my ears, and my arse landing in the mud when a two-year-old *us* stared back at me. However, this wasn't one of us, this was the essence of Mae. It was a new photo, the clothes the child wore were modern. She was sitting on the bonnet of a car, smiling widely for the shot. Her long black hair was in pigtails, and her bright blue eyes - Mae's eyes, my eyes - twinkled brightly. This year's registration on the car confirmed my thoughts.

Holy fuck.

Mae had a family. I had a niece. And the guy who had dropped in the photo was obviously her husband.

My heart burst for her, my sorrow lifting before intensifying when the reality of what she had to leave behind consumed me. She had found the very thing she had always wanted. Relief coursed through me, any taste of happiness she could have lived before passing should be celebrated. I thought I had broken her when I… when I left. Thought I had given her more of a reason to want to leave this dismal place and join our parents. And the fact that she was now with *him* agonised me.

He shouldn't be granted time with his daughter in the after-life, he didn't deserve that. The only hope I held onto was that the devil had claimed his rotten soul, and refused him sanctuary with my mother and sister.

I brushed my thumb over the happy picture, saving it to my phone as wallpaper and smiled. I wasn't alone anymore. There wasn't only me that remained of the Swift family.

I needed to find them, both her and Mae's husband. But how much had she told them? Did they think I was dead? It wasn't as if I could just walk up to them and say hi. I mean I was the exact replica of the woman they both loved and had just lost. That shit would freak them out, especially if they didn't know I existed.

But I would find them. I needed that little girl in my life more than I needed to breathe. I needed a reason to live now, and she was my only hope. I would look after her, care for her and repay

Mae for what I had done.

CHAPTER ONE

'Like mother, like daughter.'

2 Years later

Daniel

"DADDY!"

"Yeah," I shouted through the house as I pulled the bread rolls from the oven.

"Uhh...."

That single word made every single hair on the back of my neck snap to attention. I froze, the baking tray burning through the oven gloves until the scorch became too much and I tossed it on the hob. "Annie?"

"Uhh…"

Oh, Christ! What now?

"Baby?"

"Yeah, uhh…" Her voice grew nearer as she clambered down the stairs, her lack of grace holding my heart with horror of her tripping down the damn things… and not for the first time. Annie was anything but graceful. She was what I called a whirlwind; a gust of air that knocked you sideways if you didn't see her coming. She was an explosion of energy and she stole my heart every time her cheeky smile and bright blue eyes caught my attention.

It hadn't been easy. Fuck, raising her had been the most terrifying thing I had ever done, but damn, she filled the hole that had been inside me, and she continued to fill it up every second of every day.

She walked through the door – well I presumed it to be her. She had morphed into a huge ball of candyfloss, white foam covering her from head to toe, with just a peek of her eyes poking through where she had wiped at her face to see, and a few toes stuck through the bottom of the cotton ball. "Annie?"

"Right," she started, pronouncing her R with a W. "Just listen." I crushed my bottom lip with my teeth as I tried to hold onto both my sanity and amusement.

"I'm listening, Annie. I'm listening very well."

"Uh-huh." She looked up at me through the two holes and I watched as the foam shifted over her face.

"There's no use giving me your 'forgive me' grin, Annie. I can't see it."

"Oh." She nodded then exhaled heavily, the current of air through her nostrils generating little bubbles in the froth. "Well, see I was brushing my teeth, Daddy."

"With shaving foam?"

She tutted loudly, "No, silly." Her little head shook from side to side. "With toothpaste. But the mirror was dirty and I couldn't see if they were sparkly clean."

I sighed and stared at her. "So you cleaned the mirror with my shaving foam."

She nodded frantically. "But… I dunno what I did, Daddy. The bottle… it…"

"Exploded?"

"Yeah," she finished on a whisper.

I sighed and looked over her once more. "You do know that Daddy now needs to punish you, Annie?"

Her little gasp finally brought on my smile. She took a couple of steps backwards and shook her head rapidly. "No, Daddy."

"Yes, I'm afraid so Annie." She scrambled backwards when I took a step towards her, then screamed loudly and bombed it through the house. I skidded after her, my feet sliding in the trail of foam she left behind.

I let her gain a distance before I sped up and snatched her up. She squealed loudly as I tackled her gently to the ground. Her little chunky body flipped beneath me as my fingers dug into the plump flesh and I tickled her. Her gasps, giggles and piggy snorts fuelled my soul, each one enveloping it with love and affection.

"I'm gonna tell Uncle Frank," she choked out as I continued to tickle her. "He's gonna bust your ass."

I stopped tickling her instantly and gawped at her. "What did you say, madam?"

She gave that grin again but this time, because the foam had rubbed off her face after my torture, it beamed brightly at me. "I meant to say bottom."

"I should hope you did. Ass is a naughty word, baby. And ladies should never use naughty words."

She nodded and then smiled as I tapped her nose and hauled her to her feet. "Right. Let's start again or you'll be late for nursery." I smacked her bum lightly bringing forth another delightful giggle and shooed her up the stairs. "Shower, madam."

"Yes, sir." She poked herself in the eye as she saluted me. She snapped to a stop at the bottom of the stairs and turned to me. "Umm."

I blew out a breath. "Yes?"

"Well." She beamed at me again. My whole body sagged in despair. "We may have to clean first, Daddy."

I pressed the plunger on the coffee pot when I heard the front door close and turned to face Frank as he walked in. His expression told me we needed to talk - again. I sighed and gestured to the table before placing the coffee and cups in the middle and grabbed a seat.

"You need to talk to her, Daniel. She's getting worse."

I closed my eyes and rubbed my temples when the first signs of a headache thumped across my forehead. "She's just…" I shook my head and lifted the coffee to pour. "How was she at nursery today?"

He pulled a packet of cigarettes from his inside pocket then rolled his eyes and replaced them when I glared at him. Picking up his cup, he eyed me over the rim and pursed his lips. "Apparently *Mae* wants to know how you two met."

The mouthful of coffee that had just managed to calm the tension in my stomach backfired and spluttered from my mouth with force, spraying the table and Frank's white t-shirt with brown sludge. "What the fuck?"

He sighed and leaned towards me, resting his elbows on the table. "You need to listen to what I'm telling you, Daniel. This is serious. She's adamant that her mother has been visiting her."

I closed my eyes and swallowed the lump in my throat. My breathing became difficult as my heart rate veered into dangerous ground. Panic and anguish burnt a hole though my insides as I bit back the dread. "You think I should get her tested?"

He nodded slowly and looked down to his coffee. "I've never known her be this… stubborn, Daniel. Yeah, Annie's a feisty little thing but hell, she talks with such animation that it's becoming difficult for me to determine what's real and what isn't." He leaned further towards me and placed his hand over mine. My eyes snapped up to his as the awkwardness of the situation grounded us both. "If…" He gulped back his own worry and squeezed my hand. "If Annie has… the same as Mae, then we'll deal with it. I promise you that I will carry you every step of the way."

I nodded, not knowing what to say. If Annie had… well, if she had, then I knew I couldn't go through that again. I refused to watch her die like her mother had. I wouldn't accept it and I wouldn't allow it.

We were both silent for a while, contemplating what was to come. I caught the flash of Frank's eyes in my direction every once in a while but I chose to ignore him until his next sentence made me choke on my tongue.

"Daniel. What if…. What if Annie isn't… lying?"

My eyes widened, my tongue curling with shock as my tonsils started to swell. "What the fuck, Frank?"

He shrugged and sipped at his coffee casually. "I dunno, Dan. It's just… She's unwavering, resolute that the woman with long black hair and piercing blue eyes is visiting her. She talks of their conversations. She smiles as she relays it all, Daniel. Her eyes tell me that your little girl believes in what she is telling me."

"It's just…"

"She's four," he continued, ignoring me. "They say that sometimes they can… see things we can't."

Jesus Christ. "I really hope you are joking."

He shrugged again. "Who knows."

I stood up quickly, my chair scraping across the floor tiles with a loud squeak. "MAE IS DEAD!"

He looked up at me, pain and regret on his face. "I know. I know she is but…"

"I fucking killed her, Frank. There are no buts… I watched as she died in my arms, wondering if she heard what I said to her before she went."

He nodded and gave me a remorseful smile. "I know."

I turned, palming the sink as I stared out of the back window into the garden. The wind had picked up, scattering the many dead leaves to one side of the lawn, providing an area for Annie to destroy when she came home. My heart ached. I had desperately tried to remove Mae from my heart over the past two years, forget what I had done to her, forget how I had destroyed her soul but Annie, all the constant reminders that Annie produced made it more difficult. The pain was once again starting to suffocate my spirit.

"I'll book her in with the doctor."

"Okay," Frank whispered before I heard the door close behind him.

Next door's bloody cat leapt onto the shed roof after a bird, knocking the wind chimes and creating a loud but pleasant tune. The large poplar trees that bordered one side of the garden suddenly seemed eerie as the sun crept halfway out from behind the clouds that hung heavy in the grey sky, creating long dark shadows across the deep green grass.

A shiver trickled up my spine when my imagination created a vivid image of Mae running along the sand, a red and yellow kite whipping in the air behind her. Her loud happy laughter echoed around me, the vibrant pitch bringing a small smile to my lips.

It was ridiculous, but I missed her. I had only had the pleasure of her company for a few weeks but in that short amount of time, that woman had given me more than anyone ever had. She had given me Annabelle, my beautiful daughter, but more than that she had given me an area in my heart that was clean and untouched; a fraction of pureness. She had scraped away the blackness and found the part that still beat and craved to be touched.

The hairs on the back of my neck stood to attention when I felt eyes on me. My senses shot to life as my eyes scanned the garden looking for evidence to back up the sensation. Nothing seemed off, but everything seemed *wrong*. It wasn't a crazy one-off feeling, it was a strong deep knowing. Someone had been watching me.

I knew they had gone when my body relaxed, all previous

tension draining from me. However, I grabbed the gun I had illegally stashed in a box at the top of the wardrobe and went to scope the area around the house. I knew I wouldn't find anything, they had already disappeared but I needed to tell my brain that.

The wind picked up even further, blowing the last remaining leaves off the tree and propelling them down towards the gates at the rear of the garden. I followed them, and stopped dead when I saw the pile that had already collected there.

The mound assembled ready for Annie to trample through had been pushed aside, a tell-tale sign that the gate had been opened. The rear gate was never used, it led to a dark alley I refused to let Annie go through.

Yet, for the first time in eighteen months, someone had used it.

CHAPTER TWO

'Hiding uncovers the unseen.'

Connie

"ARE YOU FUCKING crazy?"

I sighed and rolled my eyes as I peeled off my jacket and slung it over the back of the kitchen chair. Katey watched me, her furious eyes following me as I pulled open the fridge and took the milk out, opening it eagerly and gulping the contents straight from the bottle. "It would seem that way," I finally replied, wiping the milk from around my mouth with the back of my hand.

She opened her hands and gawped at me. "It's bad enough that you're now talking to Annabelle, never mind watching the husband. What the hell is wrong with you?"

"Nothing is wrong with me," I snapped as I massaged the back of my neck. I was so tired, exhausted with it all. "Katey, please."

She rubbed her face with her hands then flopped into the chair and shook her head sadly. "It's not your family to haunt,

Con. Let them be."

"I can't," I whispered.

She stared at me then sighed, rising from the chair and walking over to me with a soft smile. Her hand slid over my cheek. The softness of her touch ached my heart.

"What is it about him?" Her question was gentle, but I could hear the worry, the slight hint of jealousy in her tone.

"There is nothing about him." I tried to keep my voice calm and controlled.

She flinched slightly, the small bob in her throat alerting me to the fact she knew I was lying to her. I didn't want to lie to her. I wanted to soothe her worry, appease her anguish, but I couldn't, and she knew it.

Her forehead came to rest against mine. "I…" she started as her eyes held mine. "I just feel…" I lifted my hand and wiped my thumb across her cheek, collecting the tiny tear that slowly rolled down her face. My stomach clenched at the sight of it. I was hurting her, yet there was nothing I could do to stop it. "I just feel like you're not as… into this relationship as me, as I want you to be."

I slid my hand further up her face, running my thumb across her eye and swiping the wetness that had collected on her long lashes. "Katey… I can't…"

She swallowed heavily and smiled. "I know, Con. I know."

I leaned towards her and softly brushed my lips across her mouth, tasting her tears as she opened slightly to me and allowed me to kiss her. I was gentle, trying to show her how much she meant to me, even if I couldn't voice it.

She moaned and slid her hands around my neck, linking her fingers on the nape of mine and pulling me against her. Her soft lips grew wetter as she wept harder. She knew it was the end. Sliding my hands into the softness of her blonde curls, I attempted to give her what she wanted, what she needed but it wasn't there.

She sighed into me, her warm breath tickling the surface of my tongue before she pulled away only slightly and ran the tip of her nose down the length of mine. "Goodbye, Connie."

I squeezed my eyes closed, the pain in my chest becoming almost unbearable. "I'm so sorry, Katey."

She shook her head. "No. No, don't be. I knew... You never really let me in." She shrugged and stepped back. "It's okay." The pain on her face pulled at my heart but I had to let her go. I couldn't return what she gave and it was selfish of me to hold her back from what she could find from another. "I hope you find whatever it is you're looking for, Connie."

I nodded and smiled. "And you. And you."

I watched her unhook her coat from the hook behind the door. She turned, giving me one last smile, tears scurrying down her pretty face. "Be careful," she whispered.

I didn't hide the shock on my face. She deserved my honesty if nothing else. I gave her a nod. "You ever need me, Katey. Ever."

She smiled. "I know. Next time..." She smirked at me. "Next time, make sure you hide your gun better, honey. Not everyone is as okay with that shit as me."

I chuckled and nodded. "As I said, you ever need me."

"You'll go ninja on someone's ass. I know and thank you."

I laughed as she winked at me and pulled the door closed behind her.

The room was suddenly too quiet, loneliness once again creeping in and making my soul hurt. I hated how I hurt everyone who tried to get close to me. Yet, it was something that was out of my control. I never let them in. I couldn't allow them in. My life wasn't exactly conventional, nor was I what could be deemed as *normal*.

I met Katey around eight months ago and we'd hit it off straight away. She was beautiful, her long, lush blonde hair capturing my attention; the soft bow to her lips had made me instantly want to feel them brush over my skin. Yet, where she had fallen into the trap of emotion, I would never *feel*. I wasn't capable of feeling. My heart didn't beat anymore, it died the night after my parents died - the night I found his secret.

My phone buzzed in my pocket, making me jump and bringing me out of the self-pity I never usually allowed myself to slump into.

"I warned you."

I rolled my eyes. "And hello to you too."

"This isn't a damn movie, Connie. What the fuck are you doing?"

I was suddenly angry, my jaw clenched as tight as my fist. "How fucking dare you? My whole life has been a God damn drama. Do you really think I don't know what I'm doing?"

He scoffed and I pictured him shaking his head. "We're so close, Connie. You are going to ruin everything by getting too close."

I smiled to myself. "I'll never be close enough. I want him. You promised me him. And now, now you're telling me, what? I can't have him?"

He hesitated, weighing up his words. He was worried about my recklessness. *I* was worried about my recklessness. "No, I'm not saying that. But the girl is…"

"Her name is Annie."

"Annie," he sighed, "is too unstable."

"She's four!"

"Exactly! Think what you are doing to her."

I laughed bitterly. "I'm her aunt. I won't hurt her."

"Intentionally."

I sighed and slumped into the chair. He was right. I would hurt her when all this was over. "She'll have me when it's all over. She needs to…"

"To get to know you?" He laughed and I bit my bottom lip. "Is that what you're doing? Getting her used to you?"

I paused and closed my eyes. "Yes."

He sighed. "Jesus Christ, Connie." His tone was heavy with sympathy. I bit back the tears, they would do no good, they never did any good. "We need to move this along. Let us do this without interference. I promise you we will do everything we can to keep her out of it."

I narrowed my eyes and tipped my head, suspicion curling in my gut. "Don't do this without me."

He hesitated and I knew.

"Wait…" The line was already dead. "Fuck!" I slammed my fist on the table. "Fuck!"

I shot up from the chair, the squeal of it against the tiles grating my nerves. Snatching up my coat, I tucked what I needed into the back of my jeans. It was time. It was time to do what was needed. What I had waited two years for.

It was time to set this shit into motion, with or without the go ahead. I couldn't afford to wait. He had made it pretty clear I was now out of the loop and Daniel was mine. He'd always been mine.

It was time to make him aware of that.

CHAPTER THREE

'Ghosts and mirror images.'

Daniel

"DADDY."

I nodded, encouraging her to go ahead as I tucked the sheet in around her, cocooning her in comfort.

She swallowed and eyed me warily. I cocked my head to one side and gave her a soft smile. "It's okay, baby. Tell me."

She licked her lips and stared at me for a while. My heart started to race. I could see her anguish, it was almost suffocating. My baby was hurting, worried. I sat on the bed beside her and took her small hand in mine, running my thumb over her knuckles to soothe her. "It's okay, Annie. Tell me."

"You won't be cross?"

I shook my head. "No."

"Promise?"

I ran my finger over my chest in a cross. "Cross my heart and hope to die."

She seemed to relax with my promise. "Mummy's coming."

For the longest moment I couldn't breathe. My lungs squeaked in protest when only a trickle of air managed to find its way past the clog in my throat. My teeth chewed furiously on the inside of my cheek as I tried to control the anger that surged through me. "Mummy is dead." I didn't mean for it to come out as sternly as it did.

Annie flinched and nodded, pulling her lips into her mouth to try and stop herself from crying. "I'm sorry, Daddy."

I pinched the bridge of my nose, desperately trying to control the emotion driving my heart into a dangerous pace. "No, I'm sorry. I didn't mean to snap."

Her eyes pooled with tears, marbling the bright blue of her irises. My heart broke for her. She couldn't seem to move beyond the reasoning that Mae wasn't with us.

"Baby." I brought her fingers to my mouth and kissed them. "You have to stop this. They're just dreams, Annie. Mummy... you know where mummy is, you tend her resting place and sing to her. You know this, Annie."

She nodded. "But... It's not a dream, I pinched myself last time to make sure. She comes, Daddy. She talks to me at night. We play I Spy and talk about school, and... and... you."

I narrowed my eyes. Something wasn't right. She was adamant, enthusiastic as she spoke. "What does Mummy ask?"

She shrugged. "How you met. If you're a good daddy. Who else lives here...?"

"Baby." I snatched her hand more firmly than intended. Something was seriously wrong here. "Listen to me, Annie. Mummy knows how we met, she would not ask that of you. What does she look like?"

Her eyes widened further with my sharp tone, releasing one of her fat tears down her chubby cheek. "Like... like me. She has black hair, and pretty blue eyes." She smiled as the image of her mother played in her mind.

It didn't make sense. Mae wouldn't ask those questions. I

growled at myself. Now I was falling into the trap, believing the make-believe stories of a four-year-old girl.

"Time to sleep, Annie." I didn't know what to say to her. Everything I tried didn't work. The pit of my stomach hurt when I realised my baby could be ill, like her mother had been.

I watched her, my chest aching with so much emotion as she snuggled back down under the covers.

"Daddy?" she whispered, her large round eyes locking onto mine. I nodded. "How… how did you meet Mummy?"

I closed my eyes as the pressurised storm in my chest threatened an overload. My heart cried out as memories assaulted me. "We met at the beach, baby."

She smiled up at me. "Were you both in your bathing costumes?"

My lips twitched at her innocent excitement. "We were, and Mummy was so very beautiful."

"Did you build castles and eat ice-cream?"

"We did." I smiled back at her, believing my own lies. "And we flew a kite like we always do when we visit the seaside." Her tears subsided although mine threatened to push past the dam I had built to hold them at bay. "Now, sleep."

She nodded and screwed up her fist, kissing it, then flung it at me as was our night time ritual. I copied her actions, blowing her my own invisible kiss. "Love you to the moon," I whispered as I kissed her forehead.

"Love you to the sun."

I flicked off her lamp and walked to the window to pull her curtains closed. The rain beat hard on the window, the intensity of the summer heat driving the rain as it attempted to freshen the scorched air.

I squinted at a figure standing in the middle of the road in front of the house. What stupid person would do that? Standing in both the rain and the road? Perhaps they had a death wish.

Looking closer I figured it was a female with the curve of her hips and legs in tight jeans. Her face was down, hoody pulled over her head to shield herself from the torrent pelting down on her. Both hands were shoved into her pockets as she studied the bounce of the rain on the hot tarmac, steam rising as soon as the large drops hit the hot ground.

Everything stilled, the air physically hovering around me as particles floated as if gravity had been switched off. Air gushed from my lungs, the contents of my stomach rushing up my throat with the explosion of shock when she looked straight up at me.

Blue eyes locked onto mine, bright blue eyes that peeked out from behind a curtain of ebony hair.

A choked sob rushed from me, the tight clench of my heart crippling me. "Mae?"

"Daddy?" I shook my head and turned to Annie. She sat up in bed staring at me. "Is she here?"

"I..." The world was wrong. Time and reality shifted. She died. I'd watched her die. I held her in my arms as she took her last breath. How? *How?*

I palmed the window, wiping the condensation that had formed with my hot breath. The rain continued to rebound off the ground. The trees swayed with the breeze that had suddenly descended. Next door's cat ran from one bush to the other seeking shelter from the weather. Yet no one stood on the road, nor did they appear to be elsewhere. My eyes hunted feverishly, looking, scanning – hoping.

Nothing. No one.

I blinked once, twice, trying to focus on what wasn't there. Relief coursed through me... but so did disappointment. It was crazy, stupid. I knew she was dead. Fuck, I had killed her myself. I knew it wasn't real, but a tiny sliver of hope had formed inside me. The talk with Annie had placed images in my head. That's all it had been. But sadness started to overwhelm me, eat at my soul.

I closed my eyes, trying to see her in my mind. All that came was the woman I had seen moments ago. A ghost of my past. A hallucination that continued to torment me.

"Daddy?" Annie urged.

"No," I whispered. "No, baby. Just next door's cat again."

I needed a drink. I needed the oblivion only alcohol and sex could offer. Memories, cruel, twisted memories played on repeat in my head, threatening to drown me in their punishing torture.

"Sleep, Annie." I flicked on her nightlight and pulled the door closed behind me. I didn't look at her, I didn't want her to witness the monster her daddy was.

Because that's exactly what I was. I was the corpse of the devil himself. The sin, corrupt and ugly inside me, transforming me into something that I had fought off two years ago.

My cock pounded as visions of the cruelty I had bestowed on Mae filled my thoughts, fuelled my dark side, fed the hunger in my veins. She had been such a pleasure to train, the softness of her skin tearing so easily under my retribution, the penance of my past flowing through her own blood. She had paid for my own twisted life, paid with her blood, and finally, her life.

I poured a shot of whiskey into the tumbler, downing it in one before I refilled it. Reaching up above a high cupboard, I snatched hold of the packet of cigarettes and tugged one out with my teeth, lighting it instantly in my attempt to douse the tension growing within me.

I hissed under my breath when the smooth roundness of Mae's buttocks lifted to me, begging me for more, reaching for the pain my palm braced her body with. The heat that crept over her delicate pale flesh fired shot after shot of unbearable agony through my balls.

Her body was perfection, especially with her submission right at that very moment. I tightened my fist around my cock as I quickly dragged my hand up and down, hurrying for the release of bliss that scorched me. I'd never been so turned on in my life. The way my finger in her backside had brought her climax so loudly and intensely had amazed me. She had given in to me, taken what I gave her so innocently yet so shamelessly, the bite of debauchery and depravity lighting the darkness within her.

A forbidden moan left my mouth and she looked over her

shoulder to me, her eyes wide and so very beautiful as she watched me come over her back, my thick fluid decorating her pretty soft skin, marking her, branding her.

I blinked when the crack of the glass in my tight hold snatched me from the memories. I launched it across the room, revelling in the loud smash when it hit the wall and shattered into pieces over the hob. "Fuck you," I spat to the emptiness around me. "Fuck you, Mae Swift."

CHAPTER FOUR

' Blood is thicker than water. '

Connie

HER SLEEPING FORM tilted my lips into a much needed smile. She was so innocent and perfect, a far throw from what life offered her. My heart ached for her. She was a little girl, and as much as I knew her father loved her, she still needed a mother.

Life would be hard for her, there was no doubt about that. And like me, the chosen profession of her father would torment her soul for the rest of her life.

I quietly moved across the room, creeping close so as not to wake her. Her long charcoal lashes rested delicately on her full cheeks, her nose twitching as dreams of princesses and fairies took her to where she should play out her night times. Life sucked. And she needed the fantasy only the mind could grant her.

Drops of rain dripped from my drenched clothes, trailing a path of evidence behind me. But tonight I wasn't concerned about that, about being discovered. It was time for him to uncover who had been watching him for eighteen months. Who had learnt plenty about him. The self-centred bastard had no idea. I'd been surprised at that. A man of his stature and distinction should be more alert. The fool.

Annie whimpered in her sleep, her body twitching slightly as dragons slayed her knights and baddies stole her favourite toys. The way she squirmed brought me to her side, my fingers gently brushing the sticky hair from her damp forehead. "Sshhh, Annie."

Her eyelashes slowly lifted, her bright blue eyes blurry until she focussed on me. Her cheeks plumped as a grin lit her face. "You came!"

"I told you I would. I don't break my promises, Annie Belly."

"Don't call me that." She giggled, betraying her true love of my nickname for her.

"Annie Belly," I taunted as I tickled her ribs playfully. She squealed and I clamped my hand lightly over her mouth. "Shush, sweetie, you'll wake Daddy."

She shook her head from side to side. "Daddy won't wake, he's drunk."

I frowned, anger splurging my gut. The irresponsible bastard. It infuriated me that he was unaware of my visits to his daughter. I could be anyone and with the scumbags he'd acquainted with in his past that was a lethal risk. Even entering his house had been the most simplest of tasks, the small tool I used gaining me easy access.

"Well we should leave Daddy to sleep it off. In fact, little lady, you should be asleep."

"You're late tonight." She pouted, disappointed with my lateness cutting short our time together.

"I am. But don't you worry. I told you, soon we'll get to spend more time together. And I told you I always stand by my promise, Annie."

She smiled at me, then pushed at her duvet, scrunching it aside before she clambered onto my lap. Her little arms wrapped around my neck as she reached up and planted a kiss on my cheek. My soul swelled, my heart full of her scent.

"Will you carry on with our story?"

I nodded, manoeuvring her back under the cocoon of her bedding, tucking it around her tiny body. I waited until she pulled Herbert, her dog-eared white stuffed rabbit, under the duvet with her and smiled. "Where were we?"

"You were being chased by the toad king."

"Ahh, yes. Well let's see." I pretended to think, squinting my eyes and making a funny face. She giggled and I popped them back open dramatically. "The sun beat on my back as I ran. I ran fast, Annie, so fast my feet barely touched the ground as I raced across the arid sands of the desert. 'You will never escape' King Toad boomed, his bad breath rushing past me and whipping my long hair around my face."

Annie's wide eyes were glued to me, her mind enacting the story. The further I progressed, the further her eyelashes reached her cheek, until her soft snores halted my story telling.

I suddenly panged for Mae. Tonight would change many things. And as much as I wanted to shield Annie from the things that were to come, I knew it was too hard a task to manage. She loved her daddy, and whatever or whoever he was, I knew with my whole being that he loved her just as immensely. That fact made this harder. But as much as I hated to admit it, I needed him for what I needed to do.

I kissed Annie on the forehead, softly repositioning her bedding, and crept from her room, making sure to pull the door tightly closed so she wouldn't hear what was about to go down.

CHAPTER FIVE

' Through the looking glass we see the past.'

Daniel

MY HEAD THUMPED. However, it wasn't that that woke me. Every single hair on my body reared to attention. My blood rushed around my body as both rage and puzzlement tore through me. A foreign scent assaulted my nostrils. Darkness hindered my sight. My ears picked up the strong inhalations as my cheek bore the weight of heated, furious breaths.

The knife that crushed my windpipe caused my body to freeze in fear and rage.

"Believe me when I tell you that I would love to drag this blade across your throat right now, until the spill of your blood releases you of your past sins. I want to drink your fucking essence, savour in your death, rejoice in it until you shrivel beneath me."

Her angry but controlled voice halted my breathing. I had no doubt she meant every single word. The fact it was a woman stunned me. But it was fury that a fucking bitch was *able* to do this that made me clench my teeth.

"Who are you?" I managed to grate past the push of the blade.

"You have no idea, do you? That surprises me, Shepherd."

I was puzzled. Why would she be surprised by my lack of knowledge? "Come on," I goaded. "You know my name, I think you should show me the same courtesy."

I hissed when the knife pressed deeper, the trickle of my blood itching a route down the front of my neck. "You deserve no fucking courtesy."

"I find that easy to reciprocate with the obscenity vomiting from you. I gathered you were no lady from your blatant stupidity in doing this, but your lack of refinement proves it."

She laughed. The fucking bitch laughed at me. "I was aware of your distaste for women but I think maybe you should refrain from passing judgement, Daniel… or should I call you *Master*?"

My body tensed. Was she previous stock? Stock that had fallen into some sick twisted game plan? Some of the bidders had been what even I would call sick, and that was the only explanation to what was happening. Well, that or the whisky had been left to ferment a little too long.

"I grant you permission to call me Master, *little girl*. But can you handle that side of me?"

She scoffed and I bit my lower lip when she rammed her knee into my last vertebra, shocking my spine in agony. "Do you like little girls? Do you take from them what you take from women?"

My mind was working, trying to figure out a way out of this. The blade was pressed so tightly that I had absolutely no room to move either her or me. If I tackled her, I would lose my life. I had no choice but to wait her out, hope she slipped up.

"Were you stock? A lost lamb come to seek out her shepherd. Play wolf?"

She tensed. "Stock?"

Well her answer answered my question. "What do you want?"

I bit back the pain when she took a handful of my hair in

her fist and yanked my head back to an almost breakable position. "Hmm, redemption, forgiveness, a house with a white picket fence." The blade dug in, breaking the skin slightly. "But first… Justice."

"For what?"

"We're going to do this carefully and slowly… and fucking wisely." She pressed marginally harder, giving me a warning. "Get off the bed, but please be aware, any wrong move and you're gone, leaving me alone with your daughter."

Panic surged through me, my jaw locking. How dare this person threaten Annie? She would die before I allowed any threat to be carried out. She came looking for the master and she would find the ruthless, unforgiving death he was capable of. "Annie? Where is she?"

"Calm down, she's fine. But that all depends on how we do this."

I gave her a tiny nod, wincing at the cut of the knife into my skin with the movement. "You have my word."

She laughed again. "I don't hold much on that promise, but for now I'll have to take it."

She nudged me, motioning for me to move. We moved together, her arm snaked around my chest, her hand pressing the weapon hard against me in a silent promise. I regretted my earlier decision to bury my dark side with alcohol, the fuzz in my head hindering any fight I could have put up. I had no choice but to let her lead – for now.

She guided me to the doorway. I blinked, squinting when light flooded the room. I couldn't understand why she had switched on the light, wouldn't an assailant prefer the darkness, the shadows?

We moved across the room again, her front pushing against my back, her breasts pressing into the swell of my muscles, guiding me to where she was taking us.

I flinched when a hand covered my eyes. Her skin was soft against me, her hand quite small and only just managing to obscure my sight.

We shuffled further for a while until she stopped us. "You know not my name, nor my reason for doing this," she breathed in my ear. "But you will."

She removed her hand. I blinked to focus.

The mirror in front of me seemed to suck out my soul when my eyes landed on her behind my shoulder. Her smile was sinister, icing every single cell in my body. My pulse galloped. My eyes watered from the vision, my mind screaming in the shock that rebounded off each lobe of my brain.

"Hello, Shepherd."

"Lamb?"

She tipped her head slightly, her bright blue eyes narrowing. "Is that what you called her? Lamb?"

"Lamb." I couldn't form any other words. I wasn't sure I was still breathing. I'd gone mad. My head was shaking, my mouth wide open as I stared at the reflection. "Lamb."

Oh God, my heart hurt.

An intense throb gushed in my ears, the room blurring as my vision tunnelled until it was just Mae and me in the mirror. I closed my mouth, then reopened it, my eyes wide then small. My heart raced then dipped. My body didn't know what to do. My brain couldn't comprehend what my eyes were seeing.

She gazed at me, assessing me. Very slowly she lowered her arm, removing the threat of the knife. She knew I wouldn't hurt her. Not anymore. I'd hurt her enough and I would never grant her pain ever again.

I tuned slowly, not trusting my legs to hold me up. I couldn't decipher if she was real or a vision, yet I knew the alcohol hadn't been strong enough to give me hallucinations. She stood still, allowing my eyes to soak her up. My God, she was still perfect. Still so fucking beautiful. My eyes stole her, my soul soaking her up as my mind refreshed the images that had started to fade.

I blinked when my fingers touched the edge of her cheek. I hadn't been aware of even lifting my arm, but the sensation of her skin, her life, under my touch was incredible.

A funny noise echoed around me. I wasn't even aware where it came from. The pain in my chest threatened to choke me, to spilt open my rib cage and allow it grace against the tight restriction being forced on my heart. My breath was coming in gusts; short, then long, deep then shallow.

Her lips felt soft and full under my contact, the slight dampness to them reminding me how they felt against my own. I hadn't experienced her touch for two years. A choked sob filled the room and it wasn't until I dropped to my knees that I realised it had come from myself.

She stood above me, looking down on my weakness. I shook my head, whether it was to her or myself I wasn't sure.

"I... You..."

"How many times was she on her knees before you?" she hissed, her pitch full of disgust and hatred.

I frowned. Didn't she remember? Had time stripped her memories? I prayed for that, begged with a God I didn't believe in that she had come back to me fresh and unspoilt. I didn't want to be reminded of what I had done to her, and I hoped that she didn't either.

"Did she beg when she called you Master?"

My eyes scurried over her face, confusion rendering me immobile. I reached out, wrapping my fingers around her thigh just to feel her again. Electricity streamed into me, *life* poured into me.

She looked different to how I remembered her. I had wanted to remember every inch of her, every groove of her body, every exquisite part of her, but she had changed. I couldn't pinpoint it, what was different.

"Mae," I whispered as I ran my hand down her leg, my hold completely wrapping around her calf.

She suddenly dropped to a crouch before me, making me jerk in surprise. "Wrong!" she spat. "Look again."

I peered at her, not understanding her hatred towards me. She had told me she loved me. Had time given her reflection, given her a chance to see what I did to her?

"Look. Again."

I reared back slightly, wounded by her hostility. My eyes studied her, searching for answers.

"Oh my God," I wheezed out. My fingers were once again on her face, tracing a scar that was no longer there. "Connie."

CHAPTER SIX

'Enemies and allies.'

Connie

HE REMAINED ON his knees, staring at me in shock. His chocolate eyes swirled in confusion causing a blood vessel in his temple to swell. His adam's apple bobbed up and down, his full lips parted to cater for his erratic breathing.

"How?"

He seemed angry now, the dark blaze in his eyes piercing me with his narrow glare. I smirked, chuckling bitterly. "Well, I didn't climb out of the ground if that's what you're wondering."

He didn't answer me, but got to his feet and walked across the room, palming the bed to support his shaking legs until he shuffled round and plonked down on the edge of it. He dropped his face in his hands, the muscles across his shoulders pulling tight. It was only then I noticed his lack of clothing, apart from shorts, his bare torso looking a little too nice for my liking.

"You need to get dressed."

He didn't answer nor did he move. I strolled to his wardrobe and hunted for some clothes for him. "You need to get dressed. We need to leave." I threw some jeans and a t-shirt at him. He looked up at me when they slapped him in the head and fell to the floor beside his feet.

"What?"

His brow pinched, confusion tightening his features. His eyes dulled as he looked at me. I could see the pain in him as though looking at me was agonising. "We don't have time for this. Go get Annie."

Something snapped and his eyes narrowed. Anger morphed from puzzlement, disbelief transformed into realisation. "You!" he whispered.

"Me?"

His chest heaved as his face darkened. The bite to his bottom lip made me aware he was losing control. "It's you who has been visiting Annie."

I sighed and shook my head. "We don't have time for this shit. Be grateful I haven't fucking killed you." I took a step towards him, smiling coldly at the hatred on his face. "But you need to be aware… I'm not Mae, I won't bow down to you. Fight me, and I'll fight back."

I caught his wrist quicker than he managed to strike me, my fingers curling until I dug into his flesh. He hissed, then yanked his arm so I fell against him. Fuck, he was strong. He spun me round, pulling my arm severely until I was face down on the bed, his knee digging into the base of my spine, the strict hold on my arm pulling my shoulder painfully.

Fool!

The back of my head connected with his nose, triggering a loud grunt from him. His grip loosened with the shock, allowing me some leverage. I rammed my elbow into his ribs, winding him as he bent forward, which in turn removed his knee from my back.

He was under me in seconds, the muzzle of my gun digging into the back of his skull.

We were both panting, trying and failing to control our emotions. "You know," I spat as I brought my mouth to his ear, ramming the gun harder against his head in warning. "I should just shoot you right now. In fact, I should have shot you eighteen fucking months ago." He tossed beneath me, trying to buck me off. "I am warning you. This is not the first time I have used this." I wiggled the gun further into his hair. "And it won't be the last. Do you need to find out which bullet has your name on it? Cos' I am more than happy for us to find out. Now stop this bullshit and listen."

He grunted something which I took as an acknowledgement to carry on, even if it wasn't.

"Your…" A noise vibrated along the hairs in my ears, sending warning signals into my brain. My body stiffened and so did Daniel's. "They're here."

I jumped off him. "Get Annie." He shook his head in bewilderment. "Now!" I hissed.

"How do I know I can trust you?" He narrowed his eyes on me. "You're a ghost."

I scoffed as I slipped the door open slightly, listening and peering through the gap before turning back to him. "No Daniel. I'm a Phantom."

His puzzled expression took a little longer to develop into awareness than I thought it would have. He really was an utter fool. I nodded, confirming his racing thoughts. "Now you get it. Move – now!"

"Fuck," he hissed as he suddenly shifted behind me, both of us creeping through the door and along the hallway towards Annie. "Who gave the order?"

"You think they tell me that?" I glared at him. "Shut up. Phantoms are trained to track the lowest sounds out there. And believe me when I tell you – you are not quiet!"

We stopped outside Annie's room. I tilted my chin, silently telling him to go get her. He nodded and slipped through her door. Mumbled voices echoed from the room as a shuffle along the lower hallway grabbed my attention. Screwing the suppressor onto my gun I then reached down and slid the stiletto, a long thin blade, from my boot.

"Hurry," I whispered through the door, my gaze locked on the curve of the stairway, my eyes searching the wall for moving shadows.

"Daddy?" I heard Annie's questioning, frightened voice.

"Sshhh, baby. I promise you'll be fine but you have to be extra brave for me. You must be quiet and do as I tell you. Okay?" She must have nodded because his reply of "good girl" ached my heart. She shouldn't have to go through this. She was a child. I cursed whoever had given the order. I'd been promised Annie would be clear when this went down. The lying fuck!

I held a hand up to Daniel when he opened the door to come back out. Annie's face lit up. I managed to slap my hand over her mouth before she could talk to me. Her eyes widened, terrified and confused on my gun.

"This is the end of the story, sweetie. We need to end the toad king."

Daniel stared at me but I ignored him, my eyes holding onto Annie's as I tried to instil some sense of security and calm. She gulped but nodded. "Good girl. You are so brave. I need you to do something for me."

Her lower lip quivered but she nodded. "Okay," she whispered.

"I need you to close your eyes and don't open them until I tell you to. Can you do that?"

She nodded firmly, as though grateful for my order. "Yes."

"You are definitely getting the biggest bowl of ice-cream that your tummy can gobble up."

She smiled at me, tears trickling down her face. My stomach ate at the bile trying to force free. I slipped my hand over her face, curling a piece of her soft locks around my little finger and tugging gently. She nodded, knowing my gesture meant I had sealed a promise with her, as was our ritual.

"Okay Annie Belly, time to run, sweetie. Hold on to your

Daddy and let me see how tightly you can squeeze those eyes."
She nodded and squeezed her eyes closed. "Absolutely fantastic.
Now remember, whatever you hear or feel, you keep those tight,
as tight as can be. I promise it will be over soon. I promise, sweetie."

She gave me a firm nod. I shifted my eyes to Daniel. He was
watching our interaction closely, his eyes narrow and furious but
he gave me a nod. I slipped the pistol from the back of my jeans.
"You know how to use this?"

His brow quirked high. I nodded and passed it him, needing
to trust him. "Don't make me regret it."

He scoffed quietly. "Oh, I'll make you regret many things.
But not saving my daughter."

I secured his eyes, my lips lifting into a grin. "I'll look forward to it." I pulled in a breath, unsure how many were down
there. "Time to go."

We moved slowly towards the stairs, me halting Daniel every now and again as we passed doorways so I could make sure
they were clear. The stairs were our biggest problem, open and
exposed. Holding up a hand to still him, I crept down them one at
a time, leaving him and Annie at the top until I cleared our way.

A shadow shifted to my right. I turned, my finger pressing
the trigger quicker than he had time to turn towards me. Blood
splattered from the back of his head, throwing him into the wall.

"Shit!" I hissed to myself when the thud ricocheted off the
wall. My ears were frantic, listening as my eyes scanned furiously.
Another movement to my left. I spun, dipping into a crouch quickly as I fired at him, a hole appearing in the middle of his forehead
before my knees bent fully.

A bullet shot past me, narrowly missing my ear. I dived behind a cupboard. Snorting, I mentally thanked Daniel for fixing a
mirror to the wall. I was impressed, even though the fixture meant
nothing to him, to a Phantom it meant extra eyes.

The idiot stared down the hall as I stared at him through the mirror, watching every single move he made. My heart jumped when I saw another reflection in a doorway halfway down. "Fuck."

I blew out a breath, rearranging the knife in my hand as I inhaled slowly, focussing on every single atom in the air around me.

Life is an execution. Death is a privilege.

I concentrated on the beat of my heart, using it to regulate my breathing, allowing it to tame my pulse. Stepping out I aimed my knife with a slight bend to my arm, swiftly flicking my fingers straight as the Phantom at the end shouted out. The other one stepped out of the door as if in slow motion. My finger forced the trigger. Both bullet and knife flew to their marks, both embedding their targets at the same time, both saving my life.

"Well, shit, Shadow. Who'd have ever thought you would go rogue."

I stilled, my teeth sinking into my lower lip. My mouth dried as I turned around. Blade stood before me, his customary cruel grin on his scarred face. "You think I'm defecting because I'm protecting a child?"

He laughed and shook his head. "Life for necessity." He repeated one of the many quotes buried inside all Phantoms.

"Her life *is* a necessity, Blade."

He tutted, pouting dramatically. "Well, fuck me, who'd have thought the cold Shadow had something beating in her chest?" He ran his tongue round the inside of his cheek and smirked at me. "Oh honey." The tip of his blade ran between my breasts slowly causing my breath to pause. "I should just take you here. See what's so fascinating to him about that frigid cunt of yours."

"Aww, jealous, Blade? You never know, kill me and maybe he'll reward you with his cock in your ass instead of down your throat."

"You bitch!"

My own eyes widened as shock contorted his ugly face. He was frozen in time for a moment before his mouth dropped open and blood ran from the corner of his lips, the trail that trickled down his neck reminding me of things I didn't want reminding of. I stepped back, shock of my own rendering me stupid as Blade dropped to the floor.

My eyes locked onto Daniel who stood at the bottom of the stairs, the gun still aimed towards me. He stared at me, his eyes intense and full of glee. I narrowed mine on him, not liking the look of delight on his face with the assassin of my old friend.

Life snapped back. I nodded my thanks, refusing to voice the acknowledgement. "Where's Annie?"

He turned and made his way up the stairs, reappearing a few moments later with his daughter in his arms. Her eyes were still clenched, her arms still hugging her teddy.

I licked my lips, trying to reapply the moisture that had evaporated when my life had flashed before me. "We need to go."

He frowned at me. "Why, they're all gone?"

I stared at him. "Are you really that stupid? There'll be more."

His face showed his dilemma, his eyes curious on me. "Why are you doing this?"

"You think I'm doing this for you?" I laughed, causing his teeth to clench together, his strong jaw showcasing his ire. "I'm doing this for Annie."

He swallowed, his eyes shifting to the bundle in his arms, his expression softening for a moment. He sighed deeply. "Fine, we get her to safety."

I nodded. "Don't worry. I have unfinished business. Don't let my love for Annie confuse you into thinking I give a damn about your outcome in all this."

He chuckled, prompting my gut to constrict with anger. "Lead the way, *Shadow.*"

I turned before I shot the bastard between the eyes, and made my way in front of them through the house, checking it was clear as we moved into the garage. I threw his own keys at him causing him to glare at me when he realised I'd lifted them without his knowledge. I smiled sweetly. "You drive."

CHAPTER SEVEN

'For each of us, there is an equal.'

Daniel

MY THROAT HURT as I gazed at her sleeping form, the wall of anguish building until it was almost painful. She was so adorable, so innocent and fresh-faced. She'd inherited her mother's looks as well as her heart.

My lips curled when she twitched her nose, something I'd been told I always did in my sleep. I brushed away the lock of hair that was being sucked in between her lips with each soft snore she produced, her tongue sneaking out to catch the tickle.

Sighing, I pulled the duvet up around her and swallowed. My gut twisted with anger when I thought of what had happened. How dare she come to my home and bring Phantoms with her? To my daughter!

I knew the organisation, but luckily, so far I had never had any dealings with them. They were ruthless and merciless, an establishment only the richest of the rich went to when they had 'associates' they needed to *disappear*. If you had a Phantom after you, you knew your life was over – simple. They were notorious for their cruel delivery of pain and torture, their assassins brutal and heartless.

And now, now I shared a hotel room with one.

Connie stood in front of the giant window, her arms pulled around the front of her body as she hugged herself. A deep sigh rattled from her. "Is she sleeping?"

I furrowed my brow, amazed that she had heard me from such a distance. "Yes."

She nodded without turning. I closed the distance swiftly, my anger controlling my need to hurt her but as I neared her she spun round and tutted. "Daniel." She sighed and shook her head. "You need to understand that whatever hatred you have for me, you cannot match the intensity of mine towards you. But whereas you prefer to strike out to rid you of yours, I prefer the more sensible approach."

"And that is?"

Her eyes held mine for a moment before a small smile touched her lips, the mirror image of Mae's smile pulling deep inside me. "Discipline. You should be good at that. After all, you demand it from everyone around you. But I must say," she continued after another loud tut, "you're very much undisciplined yourself."

She lifted a brow, mocking me when I chewed on my lower lip to prevent myself from launching her through the glass at her back. My veins tightened in fury as my body tensed.

"I rest my case," she murmured with a roll of her eyes before turning her back on me. My hand shot out, just missing the grasp of her hair, the air from its gentle sway echoing over my fingers. I remained stock still so I didn't lose control and throttle the mirror image of Mae, of Annie.

Walking over to the mini-bar, she dipped her body, studying the contents before selecting a mini bottle of vodka. Unscrewing the cap she devoured the alcohol in one. I watched her fill the empty bottle with water, screw the lid back on then slip it into her backpack.

"You're stealing a bottle?"

She winked at me as she reached down and unbuckled her boots. Sitting on the edge of the bed, she groaned when she pulled them off and wriggled her toes. "Isn't it a bastard when your feet hurt?"

My fists clenched at her vulgarity. "I am honestly finding your relationship to Mae hard to envisage."

Her body stiffened. "I'd rather we didn't talk about my sister."

I pursed my lips at her tone. "And why is that?"

She stood up in front of me, her eyes dark and fixed on mine as she unbuttoned her jeans and slid them down her legs. I kept my gaze trained on her face, a smug tilt to her lips showing she was aware of my inner fight to control my gaze. "Because, you don't deserve to ever utter her name again and if you do I'll cut out your fucking tongue."

I nodded, agreeing with her as I turned and walked over to a large wardrobe in the corner of the room. "That may be, but then again, what gives you the right? Mae thought you were dead. You abandoned her when she most needed you."

Silence descended. The atmosphere constricted around us and the slight wheeze in my lungs caused me to frown and turn. She was in front of me, blade out and pointed directly at my eye, the tip almost touching my tear duct.

"Let's not swap the sins we seek redemption for when it comes to Mae, Daniel. Nothing can save you from yours and if it wasn't for Annie, I would be your judgement, this blade cutting every piece of sin out of you, saving your black heart for last."

Her steady hand was impressive considering I was vibrating with anger, and worse, guilty from the truth of her words.

"Last warning about speaking her name." She lowered the blade, nicking my bottom lip before, as quickly as she had come at me, she retreated, slipping into bed.

Swiping the blood, sucking it from my finger, I pulled out the spare blanket that was on a high shelf and grabbed some pillows, making myself comfy in the high-backed chair to one corner of the room as I tried to fight my inner urges, my deep-rooted training of Master to the sheep, and not drag her from her bed and give her a lesson in blood for blood.

My thoughts ventured back to the house. Someone had put a price on my head and although that didn't drive fear through me, the thoughts of what would happen to Annie did. No child should lose both their parents at such a young age. I held no regard for my own life but every breath I took was for Annie, every lift and fall of my lungs was programmed so I could take care of my daughter. My blood only flowed so I could nurture an angel that had been created out of hell.

"I did what I had to," Connie whispered into the room. The pain in her voice was physical, like hands curling around my throat and making me gasp.

"What are you doing here? Why are you helping us?"

Darkness surrounded us, the only sounds apart from our own breathing were some drunken people singing their way home after a night out. A phone rang somewhere in the hotel but it was so low, my ears barely recognised it.

"I'm not here for you. If it were up to me, I would have ended your life years ago."

"I get that. But there's a reason you haven't yet. And I know that if a Phantom wants me dead then I shouldn't bother ordering groceries next week. But yet…"

"Yet here I am, killing my friends for you."

Her words stabbed me in the gut. "They were your friends?"

She chuckled, the sound a reflection of someone who held my heart, making me swallow back the bile. "*Were*, yes. However, we all endure the agony of Satan to experience the rapture of blood."

I frowned at her strange words. "You placed a mark on your head to protect mine."

She was silent for a moment. "Go to sleep, Daniel. We have a hard day tomorrow."

"Can I ask one thing of you?" Her silence encouraged me to ask. "Whatever happens, you will protect Annie?"

"With my life."

I didn't doubt that statement. Something clicked in my head and I smiled to myself. "She's the blood you're taking on hell's wrath for."

Her swallow was loud. "Goodnight."

I nodded, aware that she couldn't see me but something told me she was more than conscious of it. The fact that I was sleeping in a room with an assassin wasn't lost but I knew if she had wanted me dead, then I wouldn't be sitting in a chair, hugging a brittle blanket to my chest.

I turned my head, listening through the open doorway for Annie's snores. My heart swelled with the sound of them and a smile touched my lips before I drifted off to dreams of a woman who refused to break free from my soul.

CHAPTER EIGHT

'Angels and Sinners.'

Connie

"ARE YOU AN angel?"

Annie's question floored me. Her wide eyes were on my face, waiting for my answer, but all I could do was blink at her. Daniel snorted from where he was still huddled in the chair as Annie and I sat on the bed watching cartoons. I flicked him a glance, my narrow eyes giving warning. I wasn't sure I could do what was needed. I was already at my tolerance limit with the arrogant fuck, and my plans now seemed more daunting than they had.

"No, Annie. I'm not an angel, sweetie. But you most definitely are."

Her brow pinched, confusion shadowing her pretty features. "But…" She huffed and twisted her lips in thought. "My daddy says you're dead. He told me that." She turned to look at Daniel angrily. The pain in his eyes caused a lump to shift from my chest up my throat.

"Annie." She turned back to me when I said her name. I sighed and took her hand in mine, my thumb stroking across her little hand to soothe her pain. "Your mummy was my sister. My twin sister." I smiled at her, encouraging my words to make sense to her. Sometimes it was hard to remember that she was only four, her attitude and aptitude way beyond her short years.

"You should have just been honest with her from the start."

My eyes shot to Daniel. Anger surged through me and the struggle to hold back and unleash many of his untruths was proving difficult in front of my niece.

"Honesty is not always the truth, Daniel. I'm sure you're aware of that. Remember how you told Annie that you and her mummy built sandcastles on the beach when you met?"

His eyes widened, his throat bobbing rapidly as he shifted his gaze between me and Annie. "How…?"

"Well, Annie Belly, your daddy didn't tell you the truth…" He shot upright off the chair. "They made little caves because your Daddy is rubbish at castles."

He stood stock still as Annie giggled, his hands fisted by his side as he glared at me. His jaw was rigid, his lip flanked by his teeth as he angrily gnawed on the flesh. I recognised the need for death and destruction in his eyes, the mirror to my soul.

I tipped my head slightly. "We must always tell every – single – detail, Daniel!"

I would never tell Annie the story of how she was created but damn him and his double standards. I had hidden my truthful identity from Annie for numerous reasons, firstly because I didn't want her disclosing who I was to Daniel and Frank, but also if I was honest with myself, I wanted her to love me, and stupid as I had been, it was the only thing I could think of at that time.

Annie turned to Daniel, her hands on her hips and her head tilted. "Don't worry, Daddy. Connie…" She smiled widely at me before turning back to her father. "Me and Connie will teach you how to make sandcastles. They're super, super easy but we need a special bucket to help you."

Daniel grinned at her, his face lighting up. I had to admit he really was quite stunning, the depth of his chocolate eyes not only hiding many secrets but holding masses of love for his daughter. Life wasn't biased; it didn't grant you what you deserved. I knew Daniel didn't deserve Annie, or Mae's love come to that, but we were given what we were given and who was I to oppose that? At the end of the day, I deserved a much bigger punishment than Daniel ever did. But I accepted that, often choosing to discipline myself rather than waiting for it to find me.

"I'm hungry," Annie said, bringing me out of my musing.

"Of course you are, you slept in rather late this morning."

She nodded but then her little face creased up. "Connie." Nodding to her, encouraging her to ask what she needed to, I noticed Daniel's eyes close with the pitch of anguish in Annie's voice. "Will they... will they come back?"

I knew she referred to the Phantoms and although I didn't want to lie to her, it was a necessity to ease her worry. "Well... for one." I took both her hands in my own and squeezed them tight. "I'm a superhero, and I promise to protect you."

Her eyes widened as a huge excited grin erupted over her pretty face. "You are?"

I nodded firmly. "I am. I have powers that will keep the baddies away. Like the Toad King, I will stop anyone from hurting you. You have to be a big, brave girl for me though. You need to listen to your daddy and me and promise me that whatever, you will be good and listen to us."

She nodded eagerly. "I will. I promise." She took a lock of my hair and twisted it around her finger, sealing her pledge. Wrapping her in my arms, I pulled her little body to mine, feeding from her love for me and strengthening my resolve to do what was needed.

"There's one thing I need you to be brave for." Her eyes narrowed, along with Daniel's. "I need you to go stay with your Auntie while your Daddy and I sort some things out."

"What the...?" Daniel spat out. "No way!" I turned to him, my eyes narrow and accusing.

"Who?" Annie asked, her confused little face staring at me.

I turned to her, giving her a reassuring smile. "Your Auntie Helen. Your daddy's sister."

CHAPTER NINE

'You don't choose family, neither does it choose you.'

Daniel

I BIT MY lip, forcing back the acid that bubbled in my gut and trying to force itself free up my throat. How dare she do this? This wasn't her choice. Although a part of me agreed with her, Helen was the safest option for Annie. Nobody knew of her, and the fact that Connie did was quite surprising.

"Did you pack Herbert?" Annie gasped as she leaned forward in her seat, her little face appearing in the gap between mine and Connie's seat.

"I did." Connie expressed quickly to appease her. "He's tucked in securely, sleeping off the adventure as we speak." Annie nodded and relaxed again, the worry on her face making my heart pang. "Annie." Connie spoke softly again. Annie looked into the mirror to her. "I promise you that you will love Auntie Helen.

She's fun and very, very good at making scrummy cakes."

My head snapped in her direction, my glare furious and full of hatred. "You've already met her?"

She sighed and snorted at the venom in my voice. "Of course I have. You don't think I would take Annie to her if I hadn't vetted her, do you?"

"I don't know anything about you. I can't believe we're even doing this." My stomach churned the closer we got to Helen's. I hadn't seen my sister in over fifteen years. I had no idea who she was anymore. "Are you sure she's capable of looking after Annie?"

"Yes," Connie said slowly as though already bored with me.

"Don't patronise me. You have no idea about my life." I wanted to take her throat beneath my palm and squeeze the fucking life out of her. "You storm in and blow things all over, yet you still expect me to follow your every word. I'm afraid you don't know me, Connie. You have no idea what I am capable of." I kept my voice quiet, hiding my ire from Annie.

Connie reached into a bag of nuts between her thighs, shifting gears with her other hand as she popped them lazily into her mouth. My patience was running thin. I couldn't wait to drop Annie off and finally show this bitch who was the one in charge here.

She finally nodded but turned her head to the side to watch a man standing on the edge of the road, his eyes watching us pass as his girlfriend bent over the grass, vomiting furiously. "We'll discuss this later." There was no tone that gave me a reading of her mood, but I noticed her finger tap the steering wheel rapidly, the tap, tap, tap annoying.

Silence descended for a while, Annie asleep in the back as Connie and I tried to deal with the close proximity of one another.

"So." I sighed, needing information and hating the quiet. "How long have you been a Phantom?" I didn't expect her to reply so when she did my eyes widened in shock at her answer.

"Ten years." It was said bluntly. I wondered if she had any

emotions, any feelings inside that cold, frigid body of hers.

"But that…" I quickly did the math in my head and stared at her. "That would mean you became a Phantom at thirteen."

"Uh-huh," she confirmed without looking at me.

Jesus Christ. My heart squeezed at the thought of a child training to become an assassin at thirteen. "Why?"

She clicked her tongue and shifted slightly in her seat, flicking a glance at Annie through the mirror. "The why doesn't concern you, nor does my past, only the now."

We remained quiet for the rest of the journey until we pulled up outside a two-storey house. It was modern and large, surprising me.

"You'd better stay here. How do I put this?" Connie said as she smirked at me and lifted an eyebrow. "Your sister doesn't like you very much."

"Yes, I'm well aware of that."

"Might be something to do with you killing your mother, eh?"

I snatched out, seizing her neck in my hold. She continued to smirk at me, regarding me with boredom as I pulled her towards me. The bitch showed no fear whatsoever, and that made her dangerous, but I pushed that thought aside, concentrating on the now like she had told me. "You know nothing about me, so keep your judgements to yourself."

She chuckled, causing me to tighten my grip. She lifted her hand, curling her fingers around my wrist. A pain so potent fired up my arm, stabbing my chest when she pushed against a certain point on the inside of my wrist. My grip loosened instantly, shocking me when she winked and moved out of my hold.

"You never learn, do you?" She tutted and shook her head in disappointment.

She said nothing more, ignoring me and heightening my anger further. Opening the rear door she took Annie in her arms and lifted her from the car.

I climbed out, needing to kiss my angel and inhale her sweet scent once more before… before whatever came to be.

Her eyes flickered open when I ran the tip of my nose down hers. "Sleep, baby. I love you to the moon."

She snuggled into Connie and gave me a faint tired smile. "Love you to the sun, Daddy."

Connie caught my eyes, anguish held in them for the first time. I swallowed back the pain threatening to tear me in two then gave her a small nod. She smiled at me, she actually smiled, causing me to stare at her. Although Mae and Connie were twins, for the first time there was something unique in Connie. She had her own soft smile, one that lifted the whole of her face, lit her eyes and took away the sadness that was forever hostage in them. I blinked, refusing the feeling that came over me, and turned, sliding back into the passenger seat of the car.

I watched them walk up the path to the house, Connie holding my daughter and pulling her little case behind her. Connie had insisted that she entered my house alone to fetch Annie's things. It had been the perfect opportunity for me to take Annie and disappear but I knew deep down that I needed Connie to end this. I couldn't put Annie in danger for the rest of our lives, forever looking over my shoulder was something I refused to do and I wouldn't do that to Annie. She deserved to witness the sun every morning with no fears, only happiness and comfort.

The door slid open and I leaned to the side to catch a glimpse of Helen, but from the angle we had parked and the bushes edging the front path, I couldn't see her. It opened wider, allowing Connie to step inside, and removing my daughter from my care.

Pain overtook every part of me with our separation. Apart from school and the times she was with Frank, I was never away from her. Anguish curled deep inside me, my throat closing in with fear. What if they found her? What if they had followed us?

I turned in my seat, scanning the road wildly. I couldn't do this, couldn't let her go.

I scrambled from the car, racing up the path. I didn't even

knock, I just flung open the door and stormed through the house, hunting for the angel who kept my inner devil at bay.

Before I reached the end of the hallway, my body was tackled from behind, my front hitting the floor with so much force the air gushed from my lungs and left me winded. The muzzle of a gun was thrust into my temple, making me wince and still.

"What the fuck, Daniel?" Connie seethed but moved off me immediately. "You stupid fool. I could have killed you!"

I clambered upright, fury ghosting me. Grabbing her arms in my hands I pushed her hard until her back met the wall with a thud. "Where is she?"

"What?"

"Annie! Where is she?" My blood bubbled with rage, my brain was starting to vibrate and my gut fuelled the hatred inside me, clenching my stomach with the need to inflict pain and suffering.

Connie stared up at me but everything about her was composed. "Daniel, calm down."

"Where – is – she?"

"She's here!" a female voice came from behind me. My past rushed at me as my mind remembered the sweet softness to her tone. My eyes closed as I savoured the sound once again.

"Daddy?"

Releasing Connie at the sound of Annie's voice, I fought to control myself. Turning, I smiled at Annie as she stood in the doorframe, Helen's arm around her shoulder, holding her close. My eyes scanned Annie, checking she was okay before they lifted to the woman beside her.

She hadn't changed a bit, even in fifteen years. Her hair was greying, laughter lines decorating her pretty face but she was still the same; still Helen, still the sister who had protected me as much as she could from a father who had bestowed destruction and hatred upon us both.

"Helen." My voice didn't seem to belong to me. My heart pounded in my chest, reminding me of the pain I had caused to both of us, the pain that had torn our connection and forever widened the chasm that separated us.

"What do you want, Daniel?" She was full of bitterness and loathing but I didn't blame her for that.

"I…" I couldn't seem to speak, the sight of her after so long triggered horrible images in my head. My mother's dead eyes staring up at me, blood pooling around her, her final gasps of life on my face. I shivered, dropping my eyes to the floor as the guilt ate me up.

"Annie will be fine with me. I will promise you that one last thing."

I lifted my gaze to hers, seeing the truth of her declaration in her eyes. I nodded. "Thank you. I know… I know I don't deserve that…"

"No you don't. But that doesn't mean Annie doesn't deserve my love and protection."

Connie stepped forward and crouched before Annie. "I promise you will love spending time with Auntie Helen. Be a good girl and I promise I'll bring daddy back to you soon." She knotted a lock of Annie's hair in her finger and nodded to confirm her oath.

Annie smiled and nodded then looked up at me. "Please be good, Daddy. Connie loves me like you do. She needs to bring you back."

My heart exploded in my chest and I choked back the sob of anguish. "I promise, baby."

She smiled wider, then kissed her palm and screwed up her fist, throwing it at me. I caught it and blew one back, casting my heart and soul with it. "I love you."

"I love you more," she whispered. Helen gave me a nod then turned Annie and led her into the house.

"She'll be fine," Connie said, making me jolt in surprise. I hadn't realised she was beside me. I turned to her, not acknowledging her words. "Okay," she continued, "let's do this shit."

What we were actually doing hadn't been divulged to me yet but I had a feeling whatever it was, I wasn't going to like it.

CHAPTER TEN

'Enemies will tell you the truths your friends would never find the courage to.'

Connie

I CLOSED THE door behind me and sighed, welcomed into yet another hotel room. Daniel stalked across the room, tossing his bag onto one of the beds. "Well, here we are again." He turned slowly, his eyes finding mine as a small devious grin curled his lips. "Yet this time we're alone."

I ran my tongue around my cheek as I tried to hold back the laughter that wanted to free itself. "Why, Master, anyone would think you had plans for us."

His brow furrowed before his eyes widened when he caught the joke. "You want to fuck, Connie?" He took a step closer, his eyes narrow, dark and heated, causing me to gawp at him with his blunt comment.

I looked around the room dramatically then sighed. "Oh, but you don't have your equipment here. I'm sure you don't know how to *fuck* without the tools you like to degrade women with."

He snorted and shook his head. "There you go again, presuming."

"Presuming?" I scoffed as I walked across the room and studied the contents of the mini-bar, pulling out a miniature bottle of vodka. "Tell me, Daniel. Which sick fucking torture device did you use on my sister?"

His face angered before his fists curled and his chest heaved. I relished the pain that fired through my cheekbone when his fist connected with it. A shiver racked my body, forcing the inner calm to ride over me, bating the fury and bringing with it a controlled vehemence.

Tilting my neck I smiled at him, bringing a small confused glint in his eye. "Finally." He frowned deeper, puzzlement stuttering his chest. "I wondered how long it would take you to show me the pain you put on Mae, how much you hurt her. And I must say…" I laughed and smirked. "I'm sure she's dealt with much worse."

My mockery of his strength ate at his fury leaving him stumped as I walked away. "What?"

I downed the vodka, then rinsed the bottle in the bathroom sink and refilled it with water. "I thought you'd be stronger than that."

He appeared in the door, his body filling the space. "You think I'm proud of how… how I hurt Mae?"

Here it came, the truth with the confusion I granted him. Worked every time.

"You tell me, Daniel." He watched as I took both of the bottles of water and dropped a microscopic tracker inside each. "What number was Mae to you?"

"What?" he barked out again, his eyes observing everything I was doing.

"Give me your phone."

He stared at me, making me repeat my request. Finally, he pulled his phone from his pocket and handed it to me. Setting the laptop on the desk, I fired it up and logged into the programme I needed, connecting a lead from it to Daniel's phone.

"Drink this." I handed him one of the bottles. His eyes widened as he laughed at me.

"Yeah okay, darling."

I rolled my eyes then downed my own water, staring at him, daring him. I then input the unique reference into the programme and started the application on his phone. A map blinked on the screen. I turned it to face him. "See the red dot... there...." I pointed my finger to the flashing red symbol that was blinking over the icon for The Galileo Hotel we were currently staying in. "That's me. Anything happens, you can find me."

"Oh." Shrugging, he drank his own cocktail as I programmed my own phone. "Forgive me, but won't it be discarded by bodily functions? And why the vodka bottle?"

I nodded, as I hacked into the hotel surveillance, checking each view the cameras gave me. "The small amount of alcohol left in the bottle triggers it into life. This will all be over before digestion takes place. And let's face it, I don't want to know where you are after all this. Or rather, I won't need to."

He narrowed his eyes and tipped his head. "And pray tell, what are your plans for all this?"

I laughed but ignored him. Walking over to the bed, I sat down and pulled off my boots before looking up at him. I bit back the hatred residing in me and gritted my teeth. "I need your help."

He stared at me then smirked with an arrogance I was now accustomed to. Anger fuelled my hatred but I pulled it back. I needed him, it was that simple. He strolled slowly over to the chair in the corner and sat down, crossing his legs and clasping his hands in his lap. "Go on."

"I'm going to kill every single one of your father's minions, then I'm going to kill him. And then... then I am going to relish in the torture of Franco Genole."

He blinked at me. I couldn't read the emotion on his face but I noticed the movement of his throat with his hard swallow. "Oh really. And how are you going to accomplish that?"

I chuckled and lowered myself onto the bed, my back sighing at the comfort beneath it. I supported my head, my hands clasped behind it. "You're going to get me in."

He was silent for a moment but I felt his eyes on me. "Even if I were to do that, you do realise your weapons will never pass their security?"

I turned my head to look at him. His gaze was hard on mine but his brow was wrinkled. "I understand. But trust me, I don't need weapons. I have hands, Daniel. I'm quite capable of using them."

He nodded. "And there's the problem that my father is in prison."

I sat upright, fixing him with a questioning expression. "What?"

"My father," he repeated. "He's in prison. He has been for the last two years."

I shook my head. "No he isn't. Your father was released two months ago."

Shock covered his face. He shot upright, his eyes wide and his lips parted. "What? No! Tony would have informed me."

Oh shit!

I closed my eyes and sighed. "Daniel. Tony is dead."

He stumbled backwards, his calves hitting the chair, causing him to fall back into it. "What?"

"He was found... how do I put this... in pieces on the rug in front of his fire." I shivered, the knowledge of how sick and twisted Robert Shepherd was elevating my need to end him.

"But..." He ran his fingers through his hair and bit his bottom lip. "But then he will know it was me who went against him."

I shook my head. "No. He thinks it was Tony all along, hence why he made it his mission to kill him so violently. As far as I'm aware, your father thinks you just disappeared with Mae to escape the bust Tony and his team did. He doesn't have a clue where you are, but he thinks you managed to get free."

"But how has he been released?"

I shrugged. "Your father knows many people, Daniel. That and the fact that the main evidence disappeared along with the undercover officer who held all that evidence. His solicitor got him out."

"How do you know all this?"

I shook my head and flicked on the kettle, hunting through the various sachets of coffee, binning the decaf shit until I found a regular brand. "It doesn't matter. I just need you to get me in."

"So…" He shook his head in bewilderment. "So I just walk back in and introduce the two of you?" His tone was full of disbelief. I chuckled as I poured hot water into both cups, then handed Daniel his.

"Nope. You offer me up as a gift. I'm the other half of Mae. The half of his determination to pour revenge on my father. He used Mae for his stupid vengeance, yet he never got it. Imagine his pleasure when his son returns, with the only chance he has to end the rage he has held for nine years."

"Do you even realise what you're asking?"

I nodded, sipping my coffee and watching him over the rim. "Yes."

"But Franco comes and goes. You could be in there for months before he even shows his face."

I shrugged. "I'm prepared to do what is needed."

"And the Phantoms?"

I smiled at him. He really was intelligent. "Don't worry about that."

"How can I not? What if they find Annie before all this is done?"

"They won't, Daniel. Don't worry about Annie," I replied, trying to appease his worry.

He sighed and stared at me. "Do you realise what goes off in there? What they will do to you? And what if my father just wants vengeance and kills you straight out?"

"He won't, he cares too much about revenge and money. He will relish in my torture, dragging out my death as long as possible."

He shook his head with incredulity. "Why is this so important to you?"

I held his gaze. "You know why."

"Mae? You are putting your own life in danger to get revenge on the people who hurt Mae. And that also includes me."

I smiled coldly at him. "It does."

He froze, reading the hidden promise in my answer. "Am I first or last on your list?" I was surprised by his brave question. He had nerve, I gave him that.

"You, *Master*. Are the very final prize."

CHAPTER ELEVEN

'Prepare for Hell's Fury and Thou shall feel God's strength.'

Daniel

I STARED AT her. "You want me to hit you?"

She rolled her eyes and tutted. "I'm finding it surprising that you're struggling with that request, Daniel. After all, isn't that your forte, to inflict as much pain upon a woman as possible?"

She was unreal. My mind was battling with her, with the memory of Mae. Okay, there, I'd said it, the thought that was causing so much conflict. "I can't."

"What?" she asked when I turned around and walked away. Fury was striking my soul, squeezing at me until it was difficult to breathe. "Why? Daniel?"

I shook my head. What the fuck was wrong with me? Deep down I wanted to crucify her, show her what pain really was. I wanted to mark her, bruise her and scar her but Mae just wouldn't stop her incessant fucking nag in my head.

"We need to do this. You need to hit me. We can't very well walk in there, me looking like a regular woman without a scratch on me. That isn't you, Daniel. Your father will expect you to hurt me."

Why wouldn't she shut up? She was driving me crazy. "You know, you're nothing like Mae."

The room seemed to shrink beneath me. I jolted when Connie suddenly appeared beside me, her face furious but her eyes were what seized my attention. A darkness had descended over the bright blue, leaving them grey and sinister. "No," she hissed. "I'm nothing like Mae. I don't own a heart or a conscience. I relish in destruction, thrive on it. It feeds me, gives me the fuel to live this sorry fucking life. But you know that, don't you Daniel, cos' you feel that too."

I squeezed my eyes closed, the need for slaughter bubbling up until I had to tighten my fists to form some sort of control.

"Mae was easy prey for you, wasn't she? Easy for you to control and destroy. Because let's face it, *Master*. You destroyed her. Annihilated her until all that was left of her was dust that was carried away by your rancid soul."

Her head snapped to the side when my knuckles connected with her cheekbone. Her nose cracked under the force of my next blow, causing her to stumble into the wall, the palms of her hand slapping on the ugly fucking wallpaper to support her.

"Good boy," she goaded when she turned back to me and wiped at the blood trickling down her face. "You have any more for me?"

"Why are you doing this?" The relief that now ran through my veins calmed the storm inside me, quietened Mae's ridicule.

She blinked, her brow creased in bewilderment. Her eyes suddenly widened and her jaw dropped. "Oh my God."

I knew she'd sussed me. I shook my head and turned away from her, refusing to let her see beneath my skin anymore.

"I'm not Mae, Daniel. You need to get past that or this will fail." Dropping my eyes to the floor, I tried to block her out, struggling with the many conflictions inside me.

"No," I whispered. "You're not."

"Did you love her?" Her voice was quiet but it was as though she screamed the words at me, slapping me with the truth of them.

Choosing to ignore her, I picked up the small bag beside the door and eventually turned back to her. "Let's go."

She continued to stare at me, her eyes accusing but delving deep inside me. She relented and gave me a nod.

I wasn't sure I was strong enough to do this again. History had the nasty habit of biting you on the arse. Well for me, I had a feeling history would more than bite; it would slaughter.

The door greeted me like the gates to the abyss, their looming structure almost suffocating me. Connie squirmed in my hold, my fingers curling tighter into her hair. Everything around me was surreal, as though I was dreaming.

A shadow passed through the window before the door swung open. Taking a deep breath, I smiled up at Pauline. Her face blanched and she took a step back, her palm on her chest as if that would stop her heart from breaking out.

"Daniel?" Her voice was low and raspy. "Daniel?" Her eyes then shifted to my gift. Her jaw dropped and her eyes widened further. "Oh my God. Mae?"

"Connie," I corrected as I pushed her forwards into the house. Connie stumbled and whimpered. I was silently impressed by her acting skills. "Mae's sister."

Pauline stared at us both, her head shaking from side to side as though the action would deny our presence. "Uhh, your father is in the study."

I nodded briskly and directed Connie along with me. Her fingers curled around mine, as though trying to prise me off. "Stop fidgeting!" I hissed at her, aware we were already being watched.

"Fuck you!"

I pulled her nearer, bringing my palm across her mouth with a sharp slap. I refused to feel the euphoria that flowed through me. This house was like a vacuum, sucking out reality and once more plunging me into the depths of its depravity. There was an essence there, almost like it possessed you as soon as you entered, influenced your every thought and twisted you into what it wanted you to be – evil.

I caught the blink of approval in Connie's eyes but I glared at her. "Control yourself."

The study door opened just as I raised my hand to knock. He stood, proud and dominant, evil and immoral. The foulness of him once again seeped into me; vile, disgusting reactions shimmered in my head, feeding me with both despair and power.

"Father."

His dark stare locked onto me, his cruel eyes reading me. I stood still letting him have his fill of me. A smile morphed his face into something quite sinister, his eyes glinting with an ominous delight. He reached out and palmed my shoulder. "Daniel. You have no idea how much concern I have held for you."

I nodded, remembering to straighten my shoulders. "And you, Father. Forgive me, I have only just learnt of your release, or I would have arrived sooner."

He shook his head. "No, no. It's been quite an adventure, son." His eyes then shifted to the prize in my hold.

"A gift, Father."

His gaze on Connie turned my stomach. Delight poured over him, a menacing joy transforming his features until his smile twisted into a grin of utter jubilation. "Well, well. I do believe this is the reflection of the one who got away."

My skin prickled, hatred curling deep. Connie twitched under me, her action a blatant order for me to keep it together.

"Connie," I said. "Mae's sister. Mae's *twin* sister."

Father chuckled, the sound depressing and disturbing. "Yes, I can see that." He lifted his eyes to mine. "Come on. We must prepare her immediately."

I followed him into the office, watching him with disgust as he immediately prepped the syringe. Connie struggled in my hold when she observed what he was doing.

"No, please," she sobbed.

"Be still!" I barked at her, pulling her to me and clamping her arms behind her when Father walked across the room to her.

He regarded her with narrow eyes. "Do you have any clue as to how much trouble your pretty little sister caused?"

I was only just holding it together. I needed to sink inside myself to deal with this. My heart was bleeding as Mae's cries and screams echoed around me. Damn this fucking house and its malevolent ghosts.

I flinched when Connie spat at him, her hatred transferring with her mucus when it slapped on my father's cheek. He pulled her from me, his yank on her hair refusing me any chance to pull her back. She curled into a ball as he rained blow after blow on her.

It was only me who witnessed the clench of her fists, the tightening of her teeth in her bottom lip. It was only me who saw her go completely lax, letting him beat her into unconsciousness. And it was only me who saw Mae sob and hurt beneath his fury.

CHAPTER TWELVE

'Feel thy sister's pain.'

Connie

I SWALLOWED BACK the bile. All I could feel was Mae in the room, her spirit around me, her inspiration supporting me as her despair simultaneously saddened me. I envisaged her strung up like I was, her weak, frail body snapping under the torture these bastards drowned her in. I was surprised she had taken so much before death granted her peace.

I wasn't sure how long I'd been there, maybe a day or two. My stomach ached with hunger, my throat dry and sore from thirst. It struck me hours ago how merciless these bastards were. A smile curled my lips when I thought of how Isaac would react to seeing his finest Phantom hung like this before a small chuckle echoed in the room when I pictured his amusement. Yeah, fuck you, Isaac.

My legs ached but the strength I had in my arms gave the pain in my shoulders only a slight niggle. Shrugging, I sighed. I'd been through worse – much, much worse. It was the wait that was pissing me off but I channelled every ounce of inner calmness I could muster and refused the grievance to find its way to the surface.

Sweat trickled down my face, even though the room was bitter cold. I licked it from my lips and turned towards the door when it slowly creaked open.

Daniel stared at me. The darkness had already descended and overtook him. I hadn't expected anything less. I knew how it worked. To feed your depravity you had to tempt the Devil.

Eventually he moved, his slow strides bringing him closer and closer. I struggled against the chain, already playing the part that was expected.

The nearer he drew, the more I saw the sheen over his eyes, the dark glaze of sin and corruption ruling him. I wondered if his father had drugged him, the difference in him from that morning shocking and intriguing.

"Hello, Connie."

I didn't answer but kept my gaze trained on him as he approached. He stood before me and dropped his eyes to roam my nakedness. A lift of his lips showed me his approval.

"Are you thirsty?" His tone was bland, almost ghostly, like his soul had fucked off and left behind a shell containing nothing but immorality and callousness.

He circled round me then stopped dead behind me. I heard his heavy swallow. Straightening my shoulders I hardened myself to his reaction, so why I flinched when he trailed a finger along one of my welts was beyond me. A shiver raced through me and I closed my eyes. His touch burned me, scorched fire through every single nerve ending.

"So," he whispered, "you're very much like your sister after all." He spoke so quietly I wasn't sure he was even talking to me. "However, I am aware that for you to butcher your own body, brutalising your own back would be somewhat of a problem." He came round to the front of me, a finger lifting my chin until I was looking at him. "Who did this?"

I quirked an eyebrow. "And you care, why?"

He chuckled. "Oh, I don't *care*. Your disfigurement lowers your value, causing us quite the problem."

I scoffed. "I'm so sorry, *Master*. I would have asked them to stop to save you the misfortune of losing a few pounds, but at the time I didn't think they cared about my opinion."

He lifted his chin, narrowing his eyes. "Training?" He whispered the word. I nodded subtly.

"To fear pain is a burden. To feed from agony is of profit."

"Mmm, well let's hope the training prepares you for the devil's wrath, Connie Swift."

I smirked at him. "I'll survive."

He tipped his head, deliberating my statement. "That remains to be seen."

I pursed my lips. "You need to be aware that Helen is under strict instruction to return Annie to me only. She is now at an undisclosed address. If I don't make it back, then you don't see your daughter again." He glared at me, anger morphing his face. "Just a small insurance policy in case you had other ideas about how this would play out."

I hissed when he punched me in the face, his furious spittle spraying over me as he made me pay for my foresight. I let him play, because after all, this was what it was compared to what I had endured at the hands of Isaac – mere child's play.

He yanked me close with a hard grip on my hair, his face an inch from mine. "You want destroying? Then let me accommodate. You'll wish you never met me."

"Oh, Daniel. I wish you'd never met Mae. Maybe she would have had something to fight for if you hadn't decimated her."

He spun round. His body was rigid and hard, the deep contours of his back muscles straining against the material of his shirt. Anger and fury poured from him, its presence smothering and crippling. Rolling his head around his shoulders he ran a finger along the many instruments lined up on the wall until he stopped at a long thin crop.

"How Mae loved this particular piece."

Fury surged through me but I closed off to it, refused to let it and him eat at me.

"Her pale skin glowed so beautifully under the thrash of leather." He turned to me, his eyes hard and full of wicked intent. "Her sweet voice as she begged me to stop was most lyrical, her cries as hypnotising as the starlings' morning chorus."

Breathe. In. Out. In. Out

"The way she arched beneath my hand. The way she came apart underneath me was quite something. Simply mesmerising."

He orbited me slowly, dragging out his vocal torture until I struggled to blink back the tears that pooled behind my eyes. His words brought visions of Mae's torture, her need for me, her want for the pain to end.

"She even asked for it. Did you know that, Connie? Begged me to hurt her."

Breathe. In. Out. In. Out.

"She craved the dark side. Needed the pain to breathe. And I had no trouble obliging her with every sick and twisted need she had."

"You bastard!"

I was almost glad when he finally ended his verbal assault and brought forth the physical. The pain from each of his lashes didn't reach into my soul like his words had. My body was trained to accept the pain and I let it flow, allowed it to empower the hatred that was always inside me, authorised each slash of agony to awaken the dormant passion inside me. I moved into each hit, taking its full strength and devouring the power it gave me.

My skin tingled, my nerve endings coming to life as my mind closed off to the world and concentrated on the adrenaline flowing through my veins. Channelling it, my training kicked in intuitively. I consumed it, let it curl around me and bring out the side of me that needed pain.

Daniel was unaware of my arousal, oblivious to the energy he was building in me. He was ignorant to the fact that the first lesson as a Phantom was the adaptation of pain, the conversion that took place in each of us until our bodies literally hummed on the rawness that slithered over us.

I was no longer breathing, I was absorbing air. My lungs didn't inflate and deflate, they just magnetised the air from around me. My body no longer felt the slice of pain, only the eruption of vigour. My mind gave me no thoughts, only a serene void.

I was no longer a person.

I was a Phantom.

CHAPTER THIRTEEN

' Hell's Pleasure.'

Daniel

I TWISTED HER hair in my fists, thrusting my dick further into her mouth. She lifted her eyes to me, adoration and the need to please in her gaze threatening to choke me. She never failed to amaze me, her mouth always open to accommodate my length, her legs sliding apart so easily when the need to fuck overtook me. In a way I had missed Demi, the easiness to her, the simplicity she offered to the sexual side of me was uncomplicated, well it was for me. She'd always had a 'soft spot' for me, always saw me as hers and although part of that was true, she never quite did it for me. The pleasure she brought from me wasn't rapturous, nor was it earth shattering but it was a release, and an easy outlet.

Her suction intensified when she felt me swell on her tongue. Her fingers clawed at my balls, her nails stroking the tight skin underneath me. Everything tightened until my cum shot forth, filling her hot little mouth, the excess of it dribbling down the edge of her mouth and dripping over her generous cleavage.

I sighed and pulled out of her mouth, tucking my cock away. I had never managed to find that shot of exquisite heat like I had with Mae. Every partner I'd had since her, and even before her, had brought me off but never with the bliss that had come with filling Mae, stretching her tight little cunt – making her bleed.

"Better?" Father asked as Demi smiled up at me. I nodded in reply but kept my gaze on Demi.

"I missed you, Master." Her whispered devotion caused me to smile. She really was quite stupid.

"And you, Demi."

She grinned, showing me the perfection of her whitened teeth, the precision to her faults. Raising to her feet, she tipped her head then left the room.

I could feel his smirk on me and I turned to look at him. He quirked an eyebrow and shook his head slowly. "Are you sure you want to do this?"

I nodded. I was more than one hundred percent fucking sure. "Absolutely. It's time now."

He sighed and shrugged. "Your choice, Daniel but completely understandable. We all like new pussy to break and even I admit that your old whore is just that, an old whore."

I chuckled and received the tumbler of whisky from him with a nod of thanks.

"Talking of fresh pussy," he continued as he settled in the chair opposite me, his eyes gleeful and secured on me. "Your gift is being received rather optimistically in the circle already."

"I thought she might. But I must admit I'm rather surprised that you intend to auction. I thought you'd have preferred a more… personal enactment of punishment."

He sighed and pursed his lips, pausing to take another sip of liquor. "To be frank, Daniel, I owe her to Franco."

My eyes snapped in his direction but I composed myself, taking a gulp of the luxury contained in my glass, making myself savour the smooth burn of my throat and drawing my shock inside. He didn't seem to notice my reaction and carried on.

"I'm somewhat… aggrieved and reasonably saddened by his decision to educate but after the Mae fiasco, what can one do?"

"And how is Franco?"

"He's very well. Business is back to near full strength. The previous *troubles*, I will admit, caused quite a bit of unease for our clients, yet they've learnt to trust me and Franco has managed to sweeten a few palms so to speak." He chuckled and eyed me proudly. "And he's very eager to meet our new guest. He was extremely happy with your reappearance, especially after the souvenir you brought with you from your travels."

"Mmm."

"I must ask though, however did you find her?"

Licking my lips I eyed him with a shrewd smile, chuckling to refine my lie. "She was quite easy prey actually. I'd had an inkling that she had, how do we say? Pulled the wool over her family's eyes. Things that didn't fit right whilst I'd been watching Mae every year. The stupid girl thought she could shroud herself from a hunter. I just picked up some leads, contacts and other means of information. Quite simple really when your quarry thinks itself safe."

He nodded in agreement. "Yes, we all suffer from being too comfortable." He stood up, walking towards me then placed his hand on my shoulder. "Well I must say, it is good to have you back."

I didn't reply. I couldn't. I didn't feel his sentiment, nor did I feel the conviction in his statement. As if to prove me right, he halted after he opened the door and turned back to me. "Oh and Daniel." I turned my head to show him my attention, as was expected, always. "This one is special. I'll be watching your training quite closely." I didn't miss the hidden message. I was on probation, from my own father. He was known for his lack of trust in anyone, especially me.

"I would expect it, Father."

Smiling, he nodded then left, pulling the door closed behind him. I blew out a breath and leaned forward, rubbing my hands over my face, wiping away the distress. I needed to be strong. I *was* strong but fuck, if I didn't see Mae everywhere in this damn place. Her ghost dominated every corner, the echo of her soft cries constantly making my cock throb. Her blood still stained the walls, her pain potent in the air.

I knew I was sick but even I was shocked at how easy it was to slip back into the role of Master as soon as my foot had crossed the threshold. This house, this business called to something inside me, it fed the hunger for carnage and violence that lived deep inside me.

For two years I had managed to bury that side of me, concentrate on the love that my daughter brought. Her gentleness and innocence had given me a chance to find a part of me I never knew had existed. Yet here I was again; sex, depravity and bloodshed growing stronger inside me every fucking second I breathed in a house that exuded sin and debauchery.

The fact that Connie had been placed for auction was a good thing, it gave us time, time to shift through this mess. She wouldn't risk slaughter until she had all her targets in one place together, the exposure that would come with killing them one by one would jeopardise the end game. So the fact that Franco was already informed was a godsend. I knew him, he wouldn't wait to deal his revenge. He would be here shortly. But until then I would relent to the calling inside me. Connie had said she would survive, and truth be told, I needed her to survive if I was to see Annie again. However, that didn't mean that the monster in me couldn't play before that time came.

I hated how fucking breath-taking her body was. Her tight, pale skin contained curves that called for the decoration of blood. Her breasts were small but firm, her dark nipples plump and perfect. Her flat stomach showed off the vigorous side to her life, her abs defined but still feminine. She was taller than Mae, surprisingly, her legs long and her thighs strong. I wouldn't be a man if I didn't picture those legs wrapped around me securely, her lithe body squirming in pain beneath me.

I circled round her, pausing and studying the many slash marks that adorned her back. The darkness inside me was satisfied by her imperfection, by the evidence of her torture. I'd heard how brutal the Phantoms' training schedule was, but to witness it was quite amazing. By the looks of her, they hadn't just whipped her into submission, they had thrashed her into a killer, completely pulverised the child in her and built a machine.

My eyes dropped to her arse, the firm roundness tight and sheer perfection. She flinched when I slid a hand over one buttock, excitement curling within me, my dick roaring to life with a simple touch.

"I'm not sure I appreciate how your body excites me, swan." I smirked at my pet name, her body stiffening when she caught it. "You have no idea how much I want to fuck you and choke you at the same time."

"And I'm not sure which I'd rather suffer."

I quirked an eyebrow at her response. She was tough, I'd give her that. Most women would start sobbing at my remark, showing their weakness. But Connie seemed to thrive under my degradation, much like Mae had.

I slid my hand around the front of her, enclosing my fingers around the front of her throat. She gasped slightly yet I wasn't sure if it was from arousal or fear. For the first time, I couldn't read the woman under my hold. I'd always had a gift at deciphering their anxiety and panic from their needs and fantasies, but Connie was a void, nothing but indifference and control in her.

"I'm predicting you're not innocent."

She snorted and turned her head to look at me over her shoulder. "And what do you class as innocent? A virgin? Or a blank canvas that you can paint with cruelty?"

Moving around her, I cupped her chin in my fingers, holding her tightly. She glared at me but still she showed no fear. I inclined towards her until my nose brushed against the tip of hers "And wouldn't you look exquisite, decorated with your own blood?"

Her tongue slid along her bottom lip, moisturising and teasing. "How about you let me down and we'll decorate the walls with your blood... *Master*."

Running my tongue up her cheek, I whispered in her ear. "You are already on the site, the bids climbing as we speak. Well done. You've become quite the trophy for many."

She laughed. "But of course, I wouldn't expect anything less. I'm quite a treasure."

"Treasure," I repeated with a small laugh. If nothing, the Swift sisters always managed to bring a smile to my face.

"And Franco?"

"On his way."

"How perfect," she breathed. The excitement in her was palpable, her hunger for bloodshed contagious. The darkness that lived in her was a revelation, a match for my own gruesome longings.

"Mmm," I replied. "But for now we must keep up appearances."

She stilled faintly but I didn't miss it. Finally a reaction that made my gut churn, thrilling the deepest part of me.

"What did you have in mind?"

I moved back, removing my body from hers. "You want to play, swan? You need release like Mae did." Her eyes fired with hatred. Excitement grew into enthusiasm, anticipation at how much this little bitch could take. I walked over to the lever on the wall and cranked it until the chain holding Connie upright lowered, giving her some respite. She thumped to her knees, her muscles screaming at her when her face contorted in pain.

"You're simply stunning when you're overcome by pain."

"And I wonder how you will look?" she retaliated with venom as she looked up at me. I chuckled, fisting a length of her hair in my hand.

Bending into her, I smiled then tutted. "Always so eager, Connie. But as I'm such a gentleman, I insist. Ladies first."

CHAPTER FOURTEEN

' Unveil the denied. '

Connie

GRITTING MY TEETH at the pain that was tightening each un-used muscle in my legs, I looked up at Daniel. He stood before me, looking down at me. I saw the depravity in his expression, the bulge in the crotch of his trousers. His fists were clenched, his forehead creased but it was the conflict in his eyes that confused me.

"I'm not Mae, Daniel."

I hissed when his fist struck me, my neck snapping as my face erupted in pain. I didn't give him the satisfaction of a reaction.

"I may resemble her but I am very much not her."

"You think I don't know that?" he spat, his eyes blazing. He was struggling with the two sides of him, the devil on one shoulder telling him to harness his cold side and grant me the pain he so wanted to dish out, yet the angel on the other, I knew haunted him with visions and memories of Mae.

"I think you're struggling to differentiate, yes."

He dropped to a crouch before me, his hand capturing my throat, his long fingers biting into my skin. "There isn't an ounce of your sister in you."

I nodded, the action restricted under his hold. "I'm glad you've noticed. So don't back down from this, from what you need to do." He frowned deeper, my words shocking him. "I can take this, Daniel. You need to hurt me, you need to show them you can still hurt and play their game."

"Do you even understand what it is you're telling me to do?"

"Yes," I answered. "Do it."

He licked his lips, his chest heaving with his excitement. "I don't play nicely, swan. I'm cruel, twisted."

"I know. I know, but if we are to reach the end goal, the game should be played accurately."

He blinked at me before he slowly closed his eyes. "The cards have been dealt." His cryptic words caused me to stare at him. "And I refuse to let you fold, Connie."

"I never quit, you'll soon learn that about me. My promise is always steadfast."

He inhaled slowly, his eyes narrowing. "And your promise to end this game with my life."

"Steadfast." I smiled inwardly when anger held him, the confusion buried under his hatred. That was more like it.

He shot upright. "Then tell me why I should assist you?"

I pulled in a breath. I hadn't wanted to reveal this part of my assignment but he needed to know, needed to understand. "Because Annie is marked."

His eyes snapped onto mine, the colour draining from his face as a choked sound caused my heart to ache. Whatever or whoever he was, he loved Annie with a passion. "What?"

"That's all I can tell you. I need to end this Daniel. Do you understand now?"

"But what does this have to do with my father and Franco?"

"Their connection to this is my …" I sighed, shifting my

knees to release some of the tension in them, the hard floor cruel. "I am restricted from what I can tell you but... we received two separate orders, one for you and one for both you and Annie."

"My father?"

"I don't know, Daniel. I'm never given the details, only the order. That's how it works, and truth be told, normally I never want to know the details. I don't need nor want to acknowledge the reason why I take someone's life, yet Isa... my Master alerted me. He... how do I say... has a soft spot for me."

He glared at me. "You're fucking your boss?"

I pushed my tongue into my cheek, puzzled by the bitterness to his tone. "My relationship is none of your concern. But be thankful for it, because if he hadn't included me in this order then we both would be none the wiser, both you and Annie would currently be residing with my sister."

His face tightened, his fury potent around us. "There is only me and Frank who are aware of Annie's existence."

"Apparently not. Now, I'm well aware of how your father works, and I'm quite concerned as to the extent of Franco's need for revenge. Do you see what I'm getting at, Daniel?"

He nodded.

"And if they are already suspicious of you, your gift of me is strengthening your commitment to them, but it will jeopardise everything if you don't play the fucking game."

Something clicked in his eyes and his lips parted as he took a long breath. "Oh my God, you haven't been watching us to hurt us."

I rolled my eyes. He really was fucking stupid at times. "No, Daniel, I haven't."

"You've been protecting us."

"Annie. I've been protecting Annie," I corrected. He dropped his gaze to the floor, many things shifting through his thoughts. "We shouldn't be discussing this here." I flicked a glance to the camera in the corner of the room. He shook his head.

"I disabled the microphone, only the visual is working."

I glared angrily. "Christ, Daniel! They'll suspect."

"No. It's fine, I did it the moment we arrived. They'll just think it broke before we even came here. I'm not sure how long we have until they find it and fix it though."

"Can they lip read?"

"What the fuck?" He stared at me with humour. "No, they can't lip read."

"Are you sure about that?" He blinked and I sighed in annoyance. "You have to cater for every eventuality, Daniel."

He nodded in surrender. "Yes, of course. One thing is bothering me though. The order. I am well aware of how the Phantom's work. You risk your own life if you don't carry out an order."

I nodded. "Yes."

"Then…?"

"I will comply with the order."

"What?!"

"Annie will… as far as they are concerned, be taken care of." His confusion was back. "She will be given a new identity, a new life after all this. I have taken care of it, don't worry."

He sighed, blowing out a relieved breath. "Thank you." I nodded. He hadn't missed that I hadn't given him the same courtesy. "You will make sure she is cared for by…"

"I have plans in place. Annie will lead a full and good life. You needn't worry."

"How can I not worry? She's my daughter, my life!"

"My promise is the only thing I can offer to put your mind at rest, but she will get through this. She will still go to school, she will still fall in love and build a family. She will still grow old with a man who will cherish her. All the things her mother was never afforded."

His eyes met mine, the despair in them matching my own. "I would have been honoured to provide Mae with all those things." His whispered words shocked me. I wasn't even sure he had intended me to hear them but I had. He swallowed, his gaze almost pleading with me to understand him.

"But you still destroyed her."

Lowering his eyes to the floor, he nodded. "Yes."

I didn't want to witness his hurt, he didn't warrant any compassion, only pain at what his past had comprised of. I shut the thoughts out, the many mocking jeers in my head that I had done worse, much worse, than him

"We need to get on with this." He snapped out of his reverie and blinked at me, giving me a small nod of acknowledgement. "What would you usually do?"

He grimaced and closed his eyes. "Connie, really, you don't…"

"Yes! I do… get over it Daniel. I need you to hate me. You need to bury Mae, drown her out and concentrate on the old part of you, the person you were before you met her. If you want Annie to live, then do this. Don't worry about me, there is nothing you can do to me that hasn't already been done. I was trained a Phantom, Daniel, and you can only imagine the things they did to me."

"But… rape," he whispered, his face holding a shameful grimace. I was shocked by his guilt. I had been told he had settled down, changed, but to be honest I had never expected it. Satan is forever a devil, and Daniel was, or had been, the darkest of the dark.

I caught his attention. "Let's just refer to it as…. Sex with a fight."

His brows shot into his hairline, a small humorous light glinting in his eyes. "Are you sure?"

Chuckling, I nodded. "Yeah, I'm ready for a release. Sex isn't all holy for me, Daniel. Sex is… fucking, a way out for the anger inside. However, I must tell you that I don't like to cuddle after."

He tried to bury the chuckle but his lips twisted. "Not even a coffee?"

"Nah, but a cigarette would be good."

"I'll see what I can do," he whispered in my ear when he reached up and unclasped the cuffs around my wrists. "I don't kiss," he added when he leaned back from me.

I grinned at him. "Two peas in a pod. Now come on, let's fight and show them what you're made of."

CHAPTER FIFTEEN

'Untold secrets.'

Daniel

I WAS STRUGGLING to hold on to my sanity as she knelt before me. Her eyes held mine, the message in them clear. She said she could handle this side of me but truth be told, she didn't actually know that side of me.

She was the complete opposite of Mae but the exact replica and my mind was finding it hard to push out the mirror image.

Connie blinked up at me, her expression both cold and compassionate. She knew. She knew what my heart held, as much as I had tried to hide it from her. And I supposed, to her, that gave us a connection. Which in a way, it did. However, she was unaware of just how much a part I had played in her sister's death. I wasn't delusional, I knew she would end me right there and then if I told her, and I agreed, I did deserve death. But I needed to get Annie to safety first, I needed to die knowing that her life could be lived to the full.

"My name is Connie Victoria Swift." I watched as Connie lifted her chin defiantly and gave me the words I needed. "I am my own person. I am the very reason your life will end when the final card is dealt." She stood up, her face full of anger. "I am the reason Mae's life took the route it did."

I stared at her, my eyes wide and unblinking. What the fuck?

"I abandoned her when she needed me most." She took another step towards me. "I am the very reason she started to self-harm. I am the cause of her inner hatred. I am the motivation she needed to destroy herself."

"What?" I hissed at her.

Her chest heaved, her own hatred at herself evident in her eyes. She hesitated, her gaze secured on mine as she spoke the words that finally snapped my restraint. "I gave her the weapon to extinguish everything she was. I left her, Daniel. I left her alone and grieving. I walked away and never – fucking – looked – back. She was weak and she was a fool."

She flew into the wall when my fist knocked her feet off the ground, her body following with a heavy thud. She scrambled up, palming the wall for support. Her face bounced off it when my foot connected with the base of her spine. "She was not weak!"

"Yes," she spat as she attempted to get up. "She was pathetic. Poor Mae," she mocked sending my rage into a dangerous level. "Always poor, poor Mae."

I grabbed a fistful of her hair, snapping her neck back harshly as I pulled her across the room. "Don't speak her fucking name again!"

"Holier than thou, Mae. That's what they called her at school. Did you know that, Daniel? Never split her fucking legs for anyone."

She stared me out as my fingers circled her throat, the compression I forced over her larynx made a strange squeak. Her pupils fired, her tongue peeked out, her chest heaved, her breasts pushing into my chest. The bitch was aroused. Well fuck!

I smirked at her. "You want to fuck, swan? You want to show

me just how fucking holy *you* are?"

The smile that lifted her lips was dirty and depraved. "There's nothing holy about the way I fuck... *Master*."

I gasped and fell back when her forehead connected with mine, the pain causing my eyes to water.

She slipped from my hold and moved behind me. Spinning round, I grabbed at her arms, lifting her and throwing her onto the bed. She bounced, her smile widening.

"You have no idea what you're goading."

She pursed her lips, her eyes hooded and teasing. "Don't make excuses for your inability to get a hard on. Just tell me, we can simply talk if you're having trouble."

Her mocking laugh caused the air in my lungs to solidify, making it difficult to breathe. Fucking bitch. She wanted the darkness, then I'd make sure she never saw light ever again.

Grabbing her ankles, I flipped her over, her firm arse making my cock harder. There was something about her that called to something deep down inside me. It wasn't just lust, it was a need, a hunger to inflict pain but at the same time I wanted to show her exactly what fucking me was about, how fucking pleasurable it could be.

She scrambled up the bed, fighting me all the way. I pulled her back down then covered her slight frame with my own, my body crushing her under me. The outline of her body fit against mine perfectly, her backside sitting seamlessly against my crotch, the dip below her shoulder blades creating a moulding for my chest, the length of her exact for our bodies to line up precisely.

Her elbow dug into my ribs but I was too far gone to feel the pain. The darkness had shadowed any rational thought about what I was doing. One of my hands pushed her face into the mattress as my other slid down my zip, freeing my raging hard on. The bitch needed to be taught a lesson, shown just who held all the fucking cards. She was a no-one, a fool who thought she could manipulate me. There was only ever one woman who had done that, and there would never be another.

Her body twisted below mine. The power I had over her was euphoric, feeding the side of me that had been buried for way too long. It felt good to hate again, cleansing to my soul. I wanted to break the bitch, destroy her underneath me. And I wanted to witness every single glorious fucking minute of her decimation.

I hooked her ankle with my foot, pulling one of her legs to the side, opening her up for me. She struggled, but only slightly. I yanked her head back so I could rest my mouth at her ear. She was gulping for breath. I hadn't realised I'd pressed her into the bed hard enough to limit her oxygen supply that much. Not that I cared.

"You think you're my equal?" She mumbled something I didn't catch. "Well let me show you just how wrong you are!"

Her back arched under me as I thrust into her. Her pussy was wet, causing me to blink in confusion. They were always dry, always, especially the first time I took them. A moan left her lips and I smiled to myself.

"Well, well." I pulled out of her and slammed back in, my hold on her hair refusing her body any movement. "Seems the pain feeds your inner slut."

She didn't speak but I held back the groan when she circled her hips beneath me. Fuck! My balls clenched as I fought to hold back my cum. Her tight pussy was a surprise, I had expected her to be slack, loose from all her previous lovers.

She freed her hands from beneath her body but I seized her wrists before she could use them to hurt me. Pulling them above her head and holding them down, I started to thrust harder and faster, my cock sinking deeper and deeper into her. Lust took over, refusing me any control over myself as I pounded her with an intensity I had no influence over. The beast inside me found the darkness, consuming it until I lost all constraint.

I squeezed my eyes closed as heat travelled up my spine. My cock throbbed from the thrill of blood pumping mercilessly, every single muscle in my body coiled tightly, begging for release and pleasure. Her moans morphed into cries as my sickness descended, twisting every thought, manipulating my perception. She begged me to stop then pleaded for me to fuck her harder. My mind crashed with the conflicting sensations, the tight grasp of her cunt as she pleaded with me to stop, the fight she attacked me with opposed her deep moans of pleasure.

"Yes," she panted as she shook her head.

Everything started to hum, reality changing the fantasy until all I could feel was nirvana, her exquisite pussy milking me for my orgasm, her erotic moans pulling my own carnal groans and the expression of bliss on her face as I fucked her harder and harder.

She took all of me as she bucked back on me. "Hurt me," she demanded as she clawed at the bedhead with her fingers but pushed back against me to pull me even deeper.

It suddenly occurred to me as my climax exploded that she'd played the game expertly, her pleads unheard by the monitors but her actions very much observed. She relished in the pain of depravity, revelled in the sweet thrill of suffering.

I pulsed inside her, emptying my corruption into her. But her own sin devoured it, her own orgasm locking me inside her as we both rode out the fever of carnality. Her scream of pleasure matched my own, each nerve ending in my body rejoicing finally at the sheer rapture of ejaculation.

A choked sound erupted from me when I recognised the thrill as something I hadn't felt for a long while. For two years.

"No!" I shook my head rapidly as I scrambled off her.

She frowned at me over her shoulder as my wide eyes stared at her. "Daniel?"

"You…" I couldn't face up to what my body relayed to me in the afterglow of climax. "You can't be that person." My system hummed, satisfaction relaxing my sated body as the lump in my throat restricted my breathing, making me lightheaded. "Why did you do that?"

Her frown deepened. "What?" She turned so she was facing me. Her firm breasts heaved with her deep inhalations, the sight making me hard again. God damn it.

"You manipulated me!"

Tipping her head to the side she eyed me warily. "I'd lost you. You had lost yourself. I did... *said* what was needed."

My body calmed slightly. "So those things you said about Mae?"

She pulled her knees up to her chest and hugged them, blinking back the tears that threatened to spill. "Daniel. You honestly think I could think those things about Mae?" The release of her tears stunned me. She was putting on a show once again for the camera, her capacity to deceive quite disconcerting.

"I don't know anything about you, Connie. I have no clue as to what your relationship with Mae was like. She had nobody, no-one at all in her life when I met her."

"When you *met* her? I think you're starting to believe your own lies, trusting fantasy. You didn't *meet* her, Daniel. You hunted her down and ruined her." Her anger was suddenly potent. Her fists tightened, her eyes narrow but she fought it back, her gaze flicking to the camera in the corner again to remind herself to keep it in control.

"I wasn't the one who abandoned her, Connie. I take my own responsibility for Mae's death, but I think it's about time you stopped living in your own fantasy."

She clicked her tongue and shook her head faintly as though she was disappointed in me. "Sometimes the choices we have to make aren't made because they are the easiest ones. And sometimes.... Sometimes we aren't given a choice in our own choices."

Her grief was suffocating. I wasn't sure if the tears that fell from her were still fake ones. "What do you mean?"

She shook her head and sighed. "I did what I had to, Daniel. Whatever I did or didn't do, I have always believed that I did the right thing. My life was lived for my sister, my heart beat for *her*. I have no regrets; guilt, very much so but I won't repent for saving her."

My feet seemed to be glued to the spot. My legs didn't feel as though they belonged to me and I reached forward, palming the edge of the bed as many thoughts rushed me at once. "Tell me one truth." Her eyes held so much pain that her gaze crushed my insides. "Did you sacrifice your life to save your sister's?"

Her gaze dropped so I didn't witness her despair as she nodded, "Yes."

I blew out the breath that had been stuck in my throat. "Who gave you over to them?"

She lifted her eyes and frowned at me. "*I* gave me to them."

"Oh my God." Her pain was overpowering and I closed my eyes to her sorrow.

"He owed too much, the evil bastard," she said quietly, retelling her tale to herself rather than me. "Mae was sleeping in her room when they came. They came for both of us but I fought them. Well, as much as I could at thirteen. Isaac, my Master, he… I don't know to be honest, he just wanted me, said I showed potential, not that I understood what he meant then. He gave me the choice and I took it without a second thought. My death was faked two years later, my father's debts were written off and Mae was free to live her life." Her tears were fluent now as she looked up at me. "I didn't know that I would destroy her anyway. If I'd have known I would never have…" She blew out, taking control again, refusing the liberation of her grief. She lifted her chin and pulled her shoulders back. "I did what I thought was right at the time."

"You refused to cheat." I whispered her sister's words to her with a small smile. "And for that, Mae would love you unconditionally."

"But don't you see? I did cheat. I cheated death, I cheated Mae's death."

"No you didn't, Connie. You just played the game with the only cards you had in your hand at that time. Anybody would have made the same decision. Giving up your own life is far from cheating, it's the most honest thing you could ever grant."

Sadness was thick and heavy around us. She nodded. "I need to be alone."

I had a feeling this was the first time she'd ever openly dealt with what she had done, her sorrow and guilt drowning her.

Standing, I gave her a nod. "I'll be back in a while."

She gave me a small smile, the hold of her eyes on mine giving me thanks. I slid my thumb across her cheekbone, wiping away the stray tear that wasn't fluid enough to make its escape. She blinked slowly, her face dark with burden but I heeded her wishes and turned away.

I didn't miss the uncontrolled sob that echoed behind the closed door when I pulled it to.

CHAPTER SIXTEEN

'We find a traitor in every corner of the soul.'

Connie

WHAT THE HELL had happened? My sobs had died down, my guilt over Mae once more pushed aside. Daniel, or rather the last hour spent with him, filled my thoughts. Telling him my secrets was both a relief but worrying. I was usually a private person and the reason I opened up was a mystery. His love for Mae astounded me. I hadn't thought him capable and if it wasn't for the fact I'd seen him struggle to separate the two of us, then I'd have still never believed it of him.

My own words had fractured something inside me, because at one time, I'd thought them. I'd crushed my own sister at school, made fun of her with the rest of the small-minded bitches. Guilt and self-hatred had been my own form of self-harm since her death. What I wouldn't give to go back and tell her the truth, tell her that I was the more insecure out of both of us. She'd been strong enough to embrace the gentle side of her, and to stick to her beliefs whereas I had been too weak to let mine be seen. I'd conformed to peer pressure, yet Mae had fought to just be herself. And that made her the toughest.

My head snapped to the door when it pushed open. A man stood in the doorway, his cold blue eyes narrow, his thin lips pulled into a cruel sneer. His head was tilted to the side as he studied me, his gaze slowly roaming over my naked body. My heart skipped a beat. I was unaware of him, my Intel hadn't included this guy and I hated being unprepared.

"Ahh." He smiled, but it was far from a welcoming one, his handsome face twisting into vicious grin. "Finally we meet."

I watched him, bracing myself as he approached. He slid his hands into his trouser pockets as he came to stand in front of me, rocking on the balls of his feet as he locked gazes with me. There was something wrong with him. He stood rigid, almost as though he'd been frozen as he regarded me. He tutted and shook his head. "It appears Daniel is losing his touch."

My eyes widened and I forced myself to sag when he snatched my throat in his hand and pulled me to the floor in front of him. "Kneel, bitch!"

Okay. Breathe. One. Two. Three....

He forced me lower until I sat back on my heels, my backside squashed under his forceful positioning.

Four. Five. Six...

I was struggling against the need to cut this bastard's throat, my teeth clenched so tight I was sure I was pushing them into my gums.

Mae. Seven. Mae. Eight. Mae. Nine. You're doing this for Mae...

"Where's your fucking discipline?" He twisted my hair severely, pulling me across the room until I was slung the rest of the way, my body colliding with a large metal pole fixed to the ceiling and floor.

The Phantom inside me was battling with need to play the game. I wanted to break this fucker's neck, rip his throat out with my fingers but I knew to get the final prize I had to succumb to what came in-between.

My eyes widened when a leather collar was wrapped around my neck and locked into place with a clasp. I pulled away from him but jerked back when the chain attached to the choker refused me any freedom. My fingers curled around it when I was yanked backwards, the bastard tightening the leash until my body was pulled up the pole, my feet leaving the floor, my body suspended from the chain.

"If you want to live then I suggest you grab onto those hand-grips."

I squinted at the pole, my eyes watering from slowly being dangled and choked. Two tiny metal bars stuck out from the pole above my head. Reaching up, I grabbed them, pulling my body with the action until the chain had some give in it, loosening the hold around my neck.

"I did wonder what all the excitement was about." I stiffened when his palm slid down the curve of my spine. "You are stunning. The scars you bare are something of a concern but I'm sure we can work around those. Although I'm intrigued as to how you got them."

"I was a stunt double for 007."

I heard his gulp as he swallowed his amusement. "Really? Then you'll be accustomed to the excitement of performance."

What the fuck was this guy on? I had to be so careful not to fight him too much, yet I wouldn't allow him to have free rein over me, the midpoint proving rather difficult to attain in my need for revenge and the schooled discipline implanted inside me from Isaac.

"Excitement of performance," I echoed. "What did you have in mind?"

My hands started to sweat making it increasingly difficult to grip the bars. He needed to hurry the fuck up with whatever he was going to do.

He was silent and I turned to look over my shoulder. My gut clenched when he twirled a small knife in his fingers, his intense gaze on my face, his thin lips showcasing his vindictiveness. "Performance is everything, don't you think Connie... or should I call you... *Shadow*."

Shit! Fuck! FUCK!!

"And to who do I owe the pleasure?" I was stalling, my brain trying to work through several scenarios as I strived to locate a plan. I winced, clamping together my teeth, as he drew the tip of the blade down my back, blood already trickling over my naked backside.

Shit!

My eyes flew around the room, hunting for anything that could give me either a plan or a way out. How the fuck had he found out? It didn't make any sense.

"You really didn't do your homework did you? And for a Queen Phantom, that surprises me."

"I think you should allow me the privilege of a name before you kill me."

"The only thing I should allow you is a very painful death," he spat as he twisted the knife into the flesh between my hip and waist. My jaw trembled with the pain but I locked it down, concentrated on the adrenaline. The vitality coursing through my veins enlivened the Phantom inside me; every thought, every sensation and each single breath pushed aside to make way for the assassin to manifest. Calmness surrounded me, slowing the beat of me heart and most probably saving my life as my blood thickened and the rush slowed each bodily function.

My head fell back when he sliced another line adjacent to the first. I needed to do something quick. Concentrating on the hold of the grips, I closed my eyes and took a deep breath, my thoughts on nothing but the position of him.

"My name is Darren Trent. Ring any bells?"

Shit!

I wouldn't let the guilt consume me, not at that moment, it would destroy me. Nodding, I gave him the attention he deserved. "Did Isaac send you?"

He narrowed his eyes on me, his cold stare sending chills through me. "Isaac sent me here a long time ago. Do you know nothing?"

Confusion caused me to frown. "What? I don't understand."

I hissed when he dug the knife into more flesh, his hand twisting, burrowing it deeper until the pain became almost unbearable. I wouldn't allow myself to die before I'd enacted my revenge. I owed Mae that much.

He scoffed, leaning into me. "You know," he sighed heavily as though bored, "for husband and wife, you two really don't share pillow talk, do you?"

"Listen, Darren." I tracked the metal chain, my eyes following its length up to a metal ring secured to the ceiling then down into Darren's grip. "Blade, your brother, gave me no choice. You know how it is, kill or be killed." I slipped one hand off the pole and onto the chain above my head making sure not to pull on it.

"He wasn't sent to kill you though, was he? He was ordered to carry out an order you couldn't fucking fulfil. He was sent to fucking ASSIST YOU!"

"She's my niece and she's innocent in all this!"

He snorted. "And he was my brother and your friend." The forbidden gasp that left me fucked me off when he stabbed the blade into my shoulder. Shit, I needed to do this fast.

"Why did he send you here?"

He didn't answer until he moved in front of me – right where I needed him. He grinned smugly. "Because he knew you'd go rogue, Shadow. How does it feel to be stabbed in the back by your own husband?"

I locked him in my stare, sighing as many different emotions swirled through me. "I'm sorry, Darren. And for what it's worth, your brother was a good person and one of the best Phantoms there was."

His face contorted into fury, his attention solely on the hatred that my words initiated. "Better than you were," he bit out as he stepped forward to drive the knife into my stomach.

I swung my legs, wrapping them around his neck as I let both hands yank at the chain, pulling him up with the help of my body weight and the secure hold on his neck. The excess slack in the chain gave me enough leverage to twist and snap his neck. His dead weight wrenched the chain, his body dropping to the floor and heaving my own body upwards sharply. The choke was suffocating as my lungs struggled to cope with the restriction of air, my throat burning as I was slowly strangled. I grabbed the chain again, attempting to pull it but Darren's bulk refused me any leeway.

Fuck! I refused to die there, like that. I knew I didn't deserve much out of life, but I'd hoped death would be a little more accommodating.

Swinging towards the pole was impossible as I reached out to it with a leg. My system was starting to shut down as I clawed at the clasp on my collar. My eyes shot to Darren then zeroed in on his pocket knowing the key to the collar was in it, but he was too far away, his corpse resting on the floor. God damn! My vision blurred, my heart beat slowing as my organs started to go into shock.

"Fuck!"

Daniel rushed over to me, shifting his body under me until I was straddled on his shoulders. My lungs filled rapidly, my gasps for air sending my brain into a panic.

"Slowly, Connie. Take long slow breaths."

I knew how to breathe, stupid arsehole! I rested my hands on his head and dropped my forehead onto my hands as a wave of dizziness came over me. "Are you always this late to the party?"

He chuckled as he kicked at Darren, probably making sure he was definitely dead. "Hold onto the pole while I get the key." He directed my body back to the pole and I took hold of it once more.

He caught me when he unlocked the collar and I fell. "Fuck,"

I blew out.

"What the fuck happened?"

"We need to get out of here!"

"What?" He blinked at me, his forehead creased in puzzlement.

"They know who I am." I dropped from his hold when he lowered my feet to the floor.

"Shit. Your back."

"Superficial. Don't worry about it."

"It doesn't look superficial, Connie. They are quite deep." He turned me round to get a better look at the wounds.

"We can deal with them later. Right now, we don't have time."

He sighed, giving me a cautious look. "Are you sure. There's no other way? This will ruin everything."

I stared at him. "My death will ruin everything, Daniel. Don't worry, this doesn't change the end game, just the route we take across the board." He shrugged but nodded. "Are we clear?"

"Yeah, the house is empty." He dropped his eyes to Darren. "Well, it is now."

CHAPTER SEVENTEEN

'Surprises that disclose the True us.'

Daniel

THE DOOR SWUNG open revealing a tall woman, a mass of blonde curls pulled back into a bunch behind her head. She frowned at me then her eyes widened when they shifted to Connie who was holding on to me for support.

She rushed forward, dragging Connie's other arm over her shoulder and pulling her into the house. "Shit, Con. What the hell happened?"

"Hey." My brows rose at the soft look they exchanged, Connie's lips turning into a genuine smile, one she didn't display often. "I'm so sorry, Katey. I wouldn't have come to you but I…"

Katey flapped her hand at Connie, halting her apology. "Don't be silly." Her eyes shifted to me. My brows elevated further with the hatred she exposed. "You must be Daniel."

She didn't give me a chance to reply before she directed me through a long corridor and into a bedroom at the back of the house. "Lay her on the bed."

Connie smiled at me weakly, obviously apologising for her friend's harsh tone as I settled her on her stomach on top of the large bed. I smiled and shook my head. "It's okay."

Katey returned with various medical equipment. "Katey's a doctor," Connie explained when I watched her pull several things from a small case.

"Ahh." I nodded, finally understanding the reason she brought us here.

Katey started to cut through the back of the t-shirt I'd managed to slip over Connie's head, exposing the deep cuts, a deep sigh leaving her when she found what awaited her. "Jesus Christ, Con."

I winced when the material that had stuck to her skin pulled at the fresh injuries causing the bleeding to start again. Katey turned to me, her eyes narrow and heated. "Do you need to be here?"

I stared at her, humour touching my lips.

"Katey," Connie said softly, her head turning so she could look at Katey over her shoulder. She reached out her hand, Katey linking her fingers through Connie's. "It's okay, love. He's okay."

Katey lifted a brow, disputing Connie's declaration. "I doubt that but for now I'd prefer it if he left me to work."

Connie's eyes swung to mine, asking the question Katey hadn't the decency to ask me herself. I lifted my hands and shrugged. "Sure."

"Can you fetch my things from the car?" She gave me another apologetic smile.

"Sure." I blew out an irritated breath as I left them to it.

I was drinking coffee when Katey walked in to the kitchen. "She okay?"

She didn't answer me straight away, her rigid body walking past me to the sink and filling a glass of water. I kept my gaze on her, her hostility making me guarded. She palmed the edge of the sink, her back to me as she looked out of the window.

"Did you sleep with her?"

"Did *you*?"

"I don't think that's any of your concern," she spat.

I tipped my head. "You just answered your own question." It was obvious she was in love with Connie. Their relationship surprised me but on the other hand, it didn't. Connie was one of those that took sex for what it was – sex, a way to please and release tension. It wasn't sentimental for her, nor was it personal. She took it as it came, and in a way I admired her for that. Emotions just got in the way, as I'd found out with Mae.

She turned around, her eyes both angry and sad. "Did you do that to her?"

I laughed, causing her to bite her lip. "No. No, I did not."

She shook her head and eyed me warily, crossing her arms over her chest. "But from what I've learnt about you, that is something that would fit your… character."

I agreed with her wholly, but not this time. "Look, we don't like each other, and that's fair enough but let's just try and get on for Connie's sake. Hopefully we won't be in your way for too long. How is she?"

She hesitated, weighing up my words before she sagged. "She's okay. She has to watch for infection. And knowing Connie, her injuries won't hold her back." I nodded in agreement. "She's sleeping at the moment." She walked towards the door but stopped and turned back to me. "I'll stay with her. Let her rest, it's what she needs right now. God knows, you've taken up enough of her nightmares."

"I'm sorry?" Her cryptic words caused her to blanch when she realised she'd said too much.

"It doesn't matter. Just let her rest for tonight."

I took a gulp of my now cold coffee and nodded. "I trust you'll heed your own directive."

"Excuse me?"

"Nothing, just... allow her some rest."

She knew what I meant; her guilty expression told me exactly what she'd hoped would happen between her and Connie tonight. My dick hardened with the thought but, strangely, my gut twisted with hatred. I blinked, pushing the feeling aside before standing and placing my cup in the sink.

"You'll find blankets in the cupboard in the hallway. Unfortunately I don't have a spare bed so the sofa will have to do."

"That's fine." I flicked her a glance. "Thank you."

"I'm not being considerate for your benefit. But Connie will expect me to play host like a good girl."

I bit back the amusement and locked her gaze. "And are you a good girl, Katey?"

She bit her tongue and huffed in anger. "No, Mr Shepherd. I am not. But given your standards... I'm fucking holy."

I chuckled, pushing out my cheek with my tongue and nodded. "I'll remember that."

She walked away, fury radiating from her. Rolling my eyes I huffed at myself. Why the hell did I always have the need to belittle women? Memories of my childhood flooded my head, my mother's sickening pleas to my father, visions of her on her knees, her hands clawing at his clothes as she begged him not to leave her. The guilt of her death was crippling but I refused it, shaking my head to eliminate the nightmares that haunted my days.

Lifting my gaze through the window, my breath stuttered as my heart locked down, my throat tightening as I spotted a tiny blue butterfly resting on the windowsill outside. I couldn't look away as it appeared to stare at me. The fact that it was dark out made my skin ripple with goosebumps, my stomach both flipping excitedly and my legs trembling with the pain capturing my breath.

"Mae?" Her name came out a choked whisper as I lifted a hand slowly. It stayed there, regarding me as I touched the glass with my finger, stunning me further. It continued to watch me for a while before it fluttered its wings and flew into the darkness.

I closed my eyes as disappointment flooded me, then sighed when I realised I was actually going crazy. Maybe it had been a moth and I was just confused. Butterflies weren't nocturnal, and the moth had probably been drawn to the light shining through the kitchen window.

I glanced at the clock on the wall. It was still early and suddenly there was somewhere I needed to be.

I didn't want to wake Connie so I grabbed my jacket and quietly closed the door behind me.

"Hello, lamb."

Annie would be heartbroken at the sight of the weeds pushing through, their ugliness marring something that we both held dear. Dropping to my knees beside the grave, I plucked them from the ground, piling them at the side of me ready for dropping them in the bin on the way out of the cemetery.

"Well." I sighed. "Your sister is not how I imagined she would be." I chuckled to myself, picturing Mae's smirk. "She acts tough though, yet something tells me that's just a muse, camouflage for the pain inside."

I brushed away the pile of leaves and debris that had come to rest at the base of the headstone with the high winds we'd had recently. I frowned when my tidying uncovered a fairly fresh white lily. I scanned my surroundings as though I expected the bearer to still be there. The graveyard was quiet, it was night after all, but

I shuddered when something didn't fit. Connie had been with me for the previous few days so I knew it hadn't been her who had decorated Mae's resting place.

"Who came here?" I asked out loud then rolled my eyes. "Good God. I think I might actually be losing it." Maybe Helen had brought Annie. Yes, that seemed the most appropriate explanation. Relaxing slightly I traced the embossed wording on the stone, my skin once again touching Mae as my fingertip skimmed over her name.

"I miss you." I told her, knowing I didn't have company and could be honest. It was the only place I could be honest. I didn't know the reason why but her company always found its way inside me, giving me the freedom to liberate my thoughts and feelings.

The breeze picked up, generating a chill through me and triggering a shiver. "Do I trust her? Do I allow her to command how this goes? You know her better than me, my darling. I need your thoughts."

An emptiness enveloped me when nothing but quiet answered me. "She didn't leave you, Mae. She saved you... More than I could ever do." The lump in my throat was back. It was time to go. Kissing my fingers, I ran them over her name and smiled sadly. "I love you, lamb. I'll always love you. I still feel you, watching me," I disclosed with a shameful whisper. "You're still in here." I palmed my chest and sighed. "You'll always be here, right at the very front."

I took a step away then turned back to her. "Save a place for me, Mae. I'll be joining you very shortly."

CHAPTER EIGHTEEN

'The loneliness in company.'

Connie

I PEELED MYSELF from Katey's hold, soothing her murmured moan with a stroke of my thumb across her cheek. She sighed, falling into the deep realms of sleep once again. Her naked body held me hostage for a minute and I debated waking her for a moment. Katey was many things, amazing in the sack was one of them, however her emotions were her downfall. The thought saddened me. She deserved so much more and definitely someone who could appreciate her and love her.

The fact that my robe still hung from the back of her door hurt my heart further but I shook it off as I pulled it around me, wincing at the pull on my stitches, and tied the belt.

The house was too quiet, making me aware Daniel was not there. I flicked on the kettle while my laptop fired up then logged into the program I needed. My mouth dried when Daniel's location flashed up.

He had me so confused. His lifestyle, his *profession,* was very selfish. However, his emotions regarding Mae were conflictive to who he was. I had studied him for eighteen months, watching his moves, his relationship with Annie, his contact with women and although he never brought them home when Annie was there, he still had a tendency to go for the women with kinks, Daniel Shepherd liked to fuck with pain. Mae had been very much a gentle person so I knew she would never have had that kind of relationship. So what had been their connection because their association, especially for Daniel, had not been anything romantic?

I pulled the pre-pay phone out of my bag and connected it to a lead then into the laptop, sending its signal via several satellites to disguise our location before I dialled.

"PIC financial services," a woman's voice answered.

"Four-three-two-nine. I require a call back from management." Terminating the call I stared at the screen, my anger already rising before I even heard his voice. It rang almost immediately and I gave it a few rings just to piss him off before I connected.

"Hello, my love."

"How does divorce sound?"

His deep laugh both made me smile and heightened my fury. "Well, it sounds rather drastic."

"Drastic?" I stood up, turning to focus on the garden as I tried to simmer the rage in me. "How dare you. You do know Darren tried to kill me?"

He was silent for a moment. "Really?"

"Oh yeah. Would that have pleased you? Is that what you want?"

"Now, love. You know you're talking with your emotions. If you take a moment to calm down…"

"Fuck you, Isaac. How the hell do you expect me to be calm when I find out my own husband has stabbed me in the back?"

He drew in a deep breath, a slight hiss vibrating through the phone. "I suggest you calm down. I have not misled you. You're seeing things that aren't there."

"He tried – to – kill – me, Isaac."

"Yes. And maybe that's because you killed Blade. You know if that was any other Phantom, their lives would already be over. I will not tolerate that kind of behaviour, and you of all people know that. You... *YOU,* Connie, turned on your own for someone who deserves nothing but the swiftness of your blade. You are letting your heart rule over what needs to be done. If you're having trouble finding the courage to do what is needed then return and I will send another to finish what you were supposed to have nothing to do with in the first place."

I rubbed my eyes, exhaustion suddenly overtaking me. "Isaac..."

"My love.... One moment," he spoke to someone, the sound of a soft feminine voice loud enough for me to hear through the phone.

"I'm sorry, you have company."

"No woman comes before my wife, she'll wait." I rolled my eyes, already knowing the woman would currently have her lips wrapped around Isaac's dick, making his declaration null and void when he wouldn't have to wait at all. "Listen Connie, I specifically told you not to involve yourself in this particular contract, which is the reason I sent Darren into the Shepherd house. Yet you chose to deceive me by ignoring my order. You went rogue, my love. You put them before your family."

"Annie *is* my family, Isaac. She's the only blood I have left. I can't... and *won't* carry out that particular side of the contract."

He sighed. "Yes, we spoke of this. All arrangements are made for her to be cared for after. As for the other part... I need to know your stance on that."

Closing my eyes, I pushed down the surge of emotion and swallowed before answering. "I will respect the order."

"Very well. For now I will leave it in your hands."

"I miss you," I whispered. Isaac was the only one who could ever talk sense into me, made things clear and uncomplicated.

I could sense his soft smile, his eyes closing when my words wrapped him up as they usually did. "And I need you home. No one sucks my cock the way you do."

I smiled, shaking my head in amusement when I heard the gasp of his female friend. "And I think you just ruined your orgasm for tonight."

"I'm sure Becca will oblige."

"I'm sure she will," I spat. Becca had been after Isaac for many years, much to my infuriation. Although we shared an open relationship, both of us having numerous other lovers, Becca was the one that caused my jealous side to rear its ugly head. She'd had a relationship with Isaac before we married when I was seventeen, but she refused to back off, forever touching and shimmying up to him.

His laughter both angered me and amused me. "You know I would never go there, Connie. She is the only one capable of hurting you and therefore the reason I refuse her."

"I know," I said quietly, hating how my jealousy chose to be so obvious. "I'm sorry."

"Good girl. Now I must go, Jem currently has her finger up my arse and I'm rather eager to finish what we started before she bails on me."

I couldn't hold back the laugh. "Well enjoy, baby. I'll see you soon."

"Yes, you will. Take care, be safe and use your head."

"I will."

I needed something stronger than coffee so I found the bottle of vodka Katey always had stashed in her freezer and made my way down the stone steps beside her house that led to the beach. The moon was large, its reflection lighting up the darkness surrounding me. It didn't reach inside me though, it couldn't, the darkness inside me was way too black.

Taking another swig of alcohol straight from the bottle I sat on the edge of the tide, the water just reaching and tickling my toes, washing away the dried blood that had dripped from me.

Life had become too complicated. Isaac had been right, this

was one job I should have refused. I knew ending Daniel would forever haunt me, I was taking away the only thing Annie had in her life. Vengeance didn't seem so important anymore, my niece was more important than my need to sleep at night. Yet I wouldn't let any other take him from her. I owed it to her to give her father an easy death. It was the least I could do but first I needed to feel Robert Shepherd and Franco Genole's blood seep through my fingers. I wanted to taste their death, feed from the pain I would inject, and watch with delight when they took their last breaths.

I was glad, in a way, that Mae no longer lived. For her to witness what I had become would be the worst thing. If I'd have known then what I did now, I would have done things differently. I would have made sure to watch over her. I hadn't only disappeared from her life, I had abandoned her, left her thinking me dead, and after the death of my parents, I should have known that no one, not even Mae, could have dealt with that in any way normally. When I had found out about her self-harm, it had torn the final part of my soul from me, making me into an even colder killer. Nothing mattered after that. No one deserved to live if my own sister suffered like she did. Why should anyone deserve to be happy when the purest of souls on this planet was full of so much pain and sadness?

I lowered my face to the water when I sensed him behind me. I was trained to be aware and his scent of mint and citrus told me who was walking down the beach towards me.

His steps were slow, his smell growing stronger only gradually, telling me he was either wary of approaching me or he was dejected, and from his earlier whereabouts, I decided it was the latter of the two conclusions.

He missed my sister as much as I did.

CHAPTER NINETEEN

'Memories and admissions.'

Daniel

SHE DIDN'T MOVE as I approached, her knees were drawn upwards, her back to me as her head tipped occasionally whenever she took a mouthful from the bottle she held. Her sadness was potent, tangible and thick in the night air.

"She was always the strongest of both of us," she said as I drew closer. Her voice was so small, her grief taking her usual confidence.

"She was the strongest person I've ever known," I agreed as I settled beside her. She held out the bottle to me and I took it, wincing at the burn of the cheap vodka.

"Whisky your thing?"

"My thing?" I asked as the echo of Mae's own words forced a memory. I smiled at her. "You know, Mae said those very words to me once."

Her eyes caught mine and I had to fight back the emotion

when I saw the absolute devastation in her. I pulled the packet of cigarettes I had just bought from my pocket and offered her one. She smiled but shook her head before I lit my own. "Can I ask you something?"

I nodded; there was nothing to hide anymore. I was well aware that Connie knew just about everything.

"What was it about her that made you fall in love?"

I blinked then stared out at the vast amount of water stretching for miles before me, the soft ripple on the surface mesmerising in the moon's image. "I'm not sure I can answer that question. There's no easy answer to it. It wasn't just her strength or her ability to see the good in everything. Neither was it her beauty or her humour, or the way her smile lit the room. Mae was... Mae. She was many things and I fell in love with every single one. There were infinite things about her and I could never in this lifetime or the next have time to describe each one. But one thing I can tell you is that she found something in me that I never knew existed. She made me love, and that in itself deserves my limitless devotion to her."

Her eyes held mine when I turned to look at her. I reached out and wiped away the tear that rolled down her cheek. "You're cold."

"Not really." I shrugged out of my jacket and placed it over her shoulders. She smiled gratefully. "I'd like that cigarette now."

I lifted a brow and gestured to the pocket with my chin. "Inside pocket." She took them out and lit one for herself, blowing out the smoke after holding it in her lungs for a long moment, her eyes closing in satisfaction. "How long since your last?"

She snorted. "About six years." She gawped at me when I plucked it from between her lips and flicked it into the ocean. "What the hell?"

"You don't need it, stick to the alcohol."

When I thought she was about to rip my throat out, she shrugged and picked up the bottle. "I remember when we were eleven, we'd just started senior school and I wore these horrible braces on my teeth," she started after swallowing a large mouthful of vodka. "Philippa Gregory had taken an instant dislike to me, picked on me something terrible." A small giggle from her brought a smile to my face, the innocent sound coming from her was quite invigorating. "This one morning, after we'd been at school for around four weeks and Mac had witnessed this bitch's never-ending bullying, Philippa opened her locker to get her books and around twenty frogs jumped out at her." Her giggle erupted into laughter at the memory.

"Mae?"

She nodded. "Yeah, I still to this day have no idea where she got them all from. Of course she denied it was her but I knew. We always shared this secret smile whenever it was mentioned after that."

I nodded, my gaze trained on the huge moon disappearing behind the edge of the water. "She had such a stunning smile."

She turned to look at me, the light from the moon highlighted her cheekbones. I hadn't noticed how sculptured they were, completely different from Mae's softer shape. "Yes, she did." She pulled in a breath then plucked the cigarette from my fingers and took a deep drag. "Did she love you, Daniel?"

I physically winced, the pain in my chest almost unbearable at her blunt question. "She said she did. However…"

"However?" she probed, handing back the smoke. Her fingers brushed against mine as I took it from her, causing her eyes to slowly lift to mine. She quirked an eyebrow and smirked. "Are we supposed to have felt something electrical then?" Her humour to lighten the situation was a Godsend and I laughed.

"Only in Mills and Boon, Connie."

She snorted. "Why am I finding it hard to visualise you as a romance reader?"

I chuckled harder. "You'll be surprised what Playboy feature nowadays. We are more open to our sexuality, our feminine side." She laughed and shook her head, taking another drink. "Talking of feminine sides," I continued. "I take it Katey feels threatened by me."

"She shouldn't. She knows I'm incapable of sentiment. She always knew but unfortunately she never quite managed to step back from that side of things."

"I never pictured you as being a… a girl who appreciated both sexes," I managed to word delicately.

She frowned at me. "Why? Sex is sex, it doesn't matter who your partner is as long as they get you to orgasm."

I shrugged. "I suppose. It's just that you seemed rather… into the rough side of things and I can't picture Katey that way."

"She isn't, not really. There are many different pleasures to sex, Daniel. Rough, gentle, fast, slow, hard, deep, kinky, vanilla… and each one is there for a reason, to find the stimulation you need at that particular time. " She turned to me and cocked her head. "I know you prefer the painful side. Now you see, I'm having difficulty working out how that side of things worked between you and Mae. You said you loved her but I find that difficult if she wasn't able to pleasure you. You are very… masculine and I know the physical side is important to you."

"Why wouldn't Mae be able to satisfy me?"

"Well, Mae was Mae, you know?"

I stared at her then nodded in understanding. "You think because your sister was a gentle person that she didn't have a kink?"

She stared at me with wide eyes. "You mean?"

"Yeah," I nodded. "Pain stimulated Mae, quite intensely actually. I have never seen someone flourish as much as she did under my hand. It was mesmerising to witness. The thrill of pain turned her into the most erotic creature. She was very conflicted by this side of her though." Sadness gripped my heart. "I just wish…"

I flinched when I felt her hand rest over mine, her fingers sliding between my own. "You wish she had had more time to explore her sexuality with you?"

"Yes. But not just that… life too. She deserved to be adored, idolised but life was cruel to her. Fuck. I was cruel to her."

I tried to snatch my hand away when the guilt became too

much but she held firm , her fingers locking around mine to stop me from pulling away. "Tell me."

I shook my head. "No, I refuse to ever go back there. What is hidden in my head would destroy my heart. I know I deserve the pain that would inflict on me but I'm a coward, Connie. I always have been. I inflict pain and misery but there's no deeper pain and sorrow than what lives inside me."

I hated the way she looked at me. I yanked my hand back harder, releasing her hold. Standing up I turned and walked away, refusing her any more access to my thoughts. They were mine, and Mae's. She would be the only one who would ever hear them and death was eagerly awaited so I could finally show her how much my guilt over her life had decimated my soul.

CHAPTER TWENTY

'The ties that bind us.'

Connie

I KISSED MY way over her flat stomach, across the bridge of her breastbone and finally to her mouth. She moaned as I slid my tongue into her mouth, tasting her own arousal. Her fingers slid into my hair as she held me to her, her soft whimpers driving me crazy.

I closed my eyes to the sun streaming through the window, its light and declaration that it was day aching my heart as what I had to do made me feel like the shittiest person on the planet.

As though sensing my guilt she sighed and pulled back, her pure blue eyes sad as she looked at me. "You're leaving me again aren't you?"

"Katey." I sighed, resting my forehead against hers. "I can't stay here. It's not safe for you."

"I'm fine. I'm safe."

"Babe, if I thought that for one second then I would curl up beside you in bed for the rest of my life. They're coming for me, and one thing I won't do is put you at risk." I stroked my thumb across her eyebrow, my eyes following its path.

The tears that pricked her eyes punctured my gut. I wished in a way that she hated me, pushed me away herself. It would be easiest, for her anyway. Times like this I hated my life, hated what I had become and what was to come. I loved Isaac, but our relationship was far from traditional. He loved me, I knew he did, yet sometimes I felt like that love was only there because I was his best, *the best* at what we did. Was I seeing love when all it was was respect and reverence?

Swinging my legs out of bed, I dropped my gaze to the floor and braced myself. "Katey. I never told you because I didn't want to hurt you."

I sensed her stiffen behind me, the ice already forming over her heart. "Con?"

Swallowing back the bile, I forced out the words to help her move on... and forget me. "I... I'm married, Katey. I've been married for six years. His name is Isaac and I love him. Well, enough not to leave him for you." I winced at my own words and how heartless they sounded. But they were far from heartless. They were the hardest words I'd ever had to say. I cared for Katey and because of that, I did what I had to do to allow her to let me go.

"What?" Her barely there whisper tore at me and I squeezed my eyes closed. She shot off the bed and stormed round to face me when I stayed still. "WHAT?"

"I'm sorry." I stood up, stepping towards her, attempting to hold her and try and alleviate her suffering but she shook her head at me. The crack of her palm slapping my cheek was loud, or maybe it could have been the splintering of my heart, either way the guilt was physical.

"Don't you touch me!" she spat as fat tears fell down her face, the torrent causing them to run off her chin and onto her bare chest. She turned quickly, her eyes hunting around the room before she snatched up my jeans and t-shirt and threw them at me.

"Get out."

"I'm sorry…"

"GET OUT!" she screamed. "And take your fuck buddy with you. I never want to see you again, hurt or not. I hope you fucking die out there, because to be honest you don't deserve to breathe."

I nodded, agreeing with her as I pulled on my clothes. The door flew open, Daniel stood there in just shorts, his impressive naked torso catching my attention for a moment as his eyes shot from Katey to me and back again. His eyebrow quirked at the scene playing out for him. I knew he thought two naked women fighting was quite a sight but I glared at him. "Get out, Daniel. Go get dressed, we're leaving."

"Yes!" Katey hissed. "Get her out of here. Did *you* know she was a married woman before you screwed her?" Her anger was suffocating but her declaration made me want to choke her myself.

His eyes darted to mine as both his brows lifted. "What?"

"Get dressed."

I flinched when one of my boots hit the side of my head, the other swiftly following and bouncing off my shoulder. I stared at Daniel, reminding him to move. He held up both hands and turned, giving me a quick glance of a blue butterfly tattoo covering the whole of his right shoulder blade. Script I couldn't read from the distance between us decorated the area underneath.

"Oh, and don't forget this!"

I hissed when my gun cracked the side of my skull. "Shit, Katey." I'd never seen this side of her. I was quietly impressed with her aggression but I wouldn't voice that judgement.

She followed me out into the hallway, watching me as I collected my things. Daniel appeared, tugging his jacket on, his eyes flicking between Katey and me. "I'll wait in the car." I nodded, thanking him with a quick look as I shoved my laptop into my bag.

"I loved you," she whispered when the door closed behind Daniel. The heartache in those simple words was torturous.

I turned to her and nodded. "I'm so sorry, Katey." I didn't

know what else to say.

"No you're not." She was quiet now, which was much worse than her heated screams. "If you were you wouldn't have hurt me. Answer me one question truthfully, because to be honest, I don't even know you do I? You never allowed me any truth about you, Connie. You hid from me, fuck, you even hide from yourself." I gave her a small nod, allowing her question. She stared at me, her eyes narrow, the pain in them crippling. "Have you ever loved, Connie?"

"Yes," I answered honestly. "Yes I have loved."

"I'm sure you believe that. But I can promise you one thing, until you have felt love, you will never be able to reciprocate that emotion and you're too hard and impenetrable to let anyone in." I watched the single and final tear trace the edge of her chin before it fell, granting her a small moment of respite. She reached out and palmed my cheek, her hand cold but the touch gentle. "What I said before, about wishing you dead… I didn't mean it. However, when you walk out of that door, I would appreciate it if you never walked back through it."

I nodded. "You are such a beautiful person, Katey." I slid both of my hands into her hair as I kissed her forehead, leaving my mouth against her skin for a moment. "You deserve the love of a good person, someone who will make you happy, give you a reason to smile and live life to the full. I'm sorry."

Placing one last and final kiss on her, I turned and walked away.

"Connie," her voice broke as I opened the door. I turned to look at her. "You deserve that too, even if you don't believe it."

I smiled sadly and nodded even though I disagreed with her. "Take care, Katey."

Daniel looked at me when I slid into the car. "Not now."

He nodded then shifted his gaze out of the window.

I drove for twelve miles before I realised his hand was on my thigh, his thumb stroking back and forth in a soothing action.

Sighing, I slung my bag on one of the twin beds. "You know, hotels suck."

He chuckled as he placed his own bag on the other bed. "They're not so bad. And hopefully it won't be for long."

My mood was foul and I glared at him. "Whatever."

"Whatever?" He stared at me, his lips twitching with his amusement. "You sound like a sixteen-year-old."

"I was never a sixteen-year-old, Daniel. My life bypassed that stage. So maybe now, at twenty three, I feel like saying it."

He looked contrite for a moment, his eyes lowering to the floor as a small sigh left him but he nodded, sensing my mood and the need for me to be alone. "I'm going to take a shower."

I bent to look in the mini-bar. Fuck it. I picked up the phone beside the bed and called room service.

The shower fired up. I gave him a moment before I opened the door and walked into the bathroom.

"Did you want something?" Daniel shouted over the glass partition.

"Yes, a piss." I didn't wait for his acknowledgement before I sat on the loo and sighed.

"You're really quite vulgar." I curled my lip, ignoring his gripe and remained silent. "Do you think we could phone Annie?" His voice was loud so I could hear him over the rush of water. I rolled my eyes; I was about four inches away. "I miss her."

I turned my gaze towards him, appreciating the compromised view of his hard body. "Me too."

Silence descended for a moment and I stared at him shower. His hands moved to his hair, his fingers rubbing at the shampoo. He settled his head back to rinse off the suds before he stilled and his face turned back to the glass. "Do you want me to leave it running?"

I blinked, his voice bringing me back to reality. "No, thank you. Breakfast first."

"You ordered breakfast?"

"I did," I answered before I flushed and left him to it.

He walked into the room just as I screwed off the whisky cap. "Breakfast?" he asked with a tilt of his mouth.

"Breakfast."

Chapter Twenty-One

Drunken truths.

Daniel

HER EYES HAD glazed over, her body the most relaxed I had ever seen it. She twiddled the bottle cap between her fingers, her stare fixed on a random point on the wall. She slid off the bottom of the bed, drew her knees up and rested her forehead against them.

"So." I cocked my head and looked at her. "Married, huh?"

"Do you ever get tired of living Daniel?" she asked, completely ignoring my query.

Her suffering was loud in the quiet of the room. Sighing, I came to sit beside her and took the bottle from her, filling my belly with the expensive liquor she'd ordered.

"All the damn time." I was feeling the effects of the whisky myself, the edges of the room less harsh, the ache in my chest a little lighter.

She nodded then turned to me. "Tell me about your childhood." Her words weren't slurred but they were slower than her usual pronunciation.

Her brow rose when I tensed. I pulled in another large draw of whisky, a huge breath then stared straight forward. "My parents hated me."

She snorted and took the bottle from me, her head nodding slightly. "I can see why." I stared at her and she winked. "Go on."

The laugh she brought on relaxed me a little and I settled further back into the bed. "Helen looked after me. My mother was a drunk, my father was a bully. In fact, he still is." I shrugged. "And that's all there is to tell."

"Bullshit. What happened with your sister, apart from the fact that killing your mother alienated her?"

"You know," I bit back the boil of anger, "you shouldn't judge people until you know their full story."

She opened her hands. "And that's what I'm trying to do. To hear your story."

"Why do you want to hear my story?" I reached towards the table and grabbed a bread roll, the only thing Connie had ordered food-wise for our breakfast.

"Because it's better than relaying mine over and over in my head." She didn't look at me but her cheeks heated faintly. She followed me, taking a roll for herself before she started to pull off small pieces and pop them into her mouth. She turned back to me, her eyes pleading. I understood her. The details of the past become undecipherable at times, the pain from it bearing down constantly until the edges merged into what your future held and all of a sudden all that was to come had already passed. I of all people understood that.

"You know that term," I said quietly. "The circle of life. Well for me, it is most appropriate." She nodded but didn't interrupt. Closing my eyes, I pulled in a deep breath. "My family was a wealthy one, or rather a greedy one. I only remember Helen from my younger years. It was her who nursed me, her who read to me, her who played games with me; my own sister became my mother."

Connie watched me when I pulled out a cigarette and lit it. She stumbled to her feet and dragged a cloth from the bathroom then proceeded to wrap it around the smoke detector before coming back to sit beside me on the floor.

"It wasn't until I was in my early teens that my father became interested in me as someone to join the business. I'll admit, without being egotistical that I was already good looking by thirteen, the attention I received from girls verified it. Home life was still turbulent and like any wayward teenager with self-confidence issues, I started to take drugs and drink heavily. I was the life and soul of any party, the *fun guy* to be around."

Connie turned towards me, resting her cheek on her knees. Her sad eyes locked onto mine as she guided me through. "But it was all a lie."

"In a way, yes but not entirely. I'd watched my father with numerous women over the years, especially my mother. Each of them worshipped him, they actually begged him to fuck them. I couldn't understand it at the time, what they saw, what they needed from him. It wasn't until I started to indulge in girls that it finally made sense. Women were, *are* a peculiar breed."

Connie snorted but nodded. "I agree."

"I'm not going to lie to you, Connie. I find pleasure in women's pain." She remained quiet, her stare on the carpet in front of us. "It confused me to begin with, the way my father treated women and their reaction to it. Some of them begged him to hurt them. I admired their honesty to what they wanted. But others denied it, fought him. These were the ones who caught my attention because at the end of the day, they also craved the pain, but they refused it. Why? Why refuse something you need?"

"Not every woman is like that Daniel. Some actually don't want that."

I laughed, shaking my head, denying her declaration. "Actually, they do. Each one, under my schooling finally found that side of themselves."

"No. You didn't liberate that side of them, you moulded them into the person you thought they were. You forced them to enjoy pain, you took their fear and turned it into lust. That isn't discovery, that's manipulation." She turned to me. She wasn't angry just insistent. "And may I add, the pain you delivered was far from sexual. You are cruel, Daniel. I've…" She pursed her lips and exhaled heavily. "I've spoken to some of the women who you sent into that sordid world."

I stared at her, shocked by her admission. "You what?"

"It doesn't matter but what I'm telling you is…"

Her throat tightened when my fingers wrapped too firmly around her neck. "What have you done?"

She was calm under the thunderstorm brewing inside me, her eyes neutral as mine blazed, her body relaxed as mine stiffened under my rage. "Let go," she hissed out.

"You had no right!"

She pushed me back with her hands, forcing our bodies onto the floor as I kept my hold on her neck. Her thighs straddled me immediately, her chest crushed against mine as I pulled her closer. Rolling our bodies over, I pinned her under me, pressing her face into the carpet. "Why did you go to them?"

"Because I needed to know what you put Mae through. They were the only ones with that information."

I leaned into her ear, my chest hard against her back as fury reigned over common sense. "This isn't some damn romance novel, swan. You expect me to give you some sob story about my family life but there isn't one. I enjoyed every single second destroying those women. I relished in the hunt, the terror on their faces when they realised their lives would never be the same again. And Mae was one of those…" Before I could finish the sentence her elbow rammed into the side of my temple. I hadn't even been aware that she'd managed to free her arms. I fell to the side, allowing her to escape my hold but before she could make her move, I rolled over and jumped up. She did the same.

We stood, eyes narrowed on each other. "I don't know what

123

you want me to tell you, Connie. I'm not a victim and you're not a Good Samaritan. You can't save me, just as much as you can't redeem yourself."

"You mistake me, Daniel," she hissed. "I'm not trying to save you. I'm going to kill you… slowly."

I didn't doubt her for one second, however if she thought I would bow down to her, a woman, then she had another think coming. Her back thumped against the wall when I circled her throat again and pushed her back with a furious strength. The white rage was back, the need to deliver agony tempting me once again.

I stared at her, hating her for what I had returned to. "Two years I have fought to abolish the need to hurt. TWO FUCKING YEARS! And you… you turn it all around in the blink of an eye." I was so damn angry. At her for having the ability to pull out the darkness in me, for unlocking and opening the doors to the beast inside, freeing him with the rage that was always present within me. At myself for craving that darkness, for needing it with an intolerable hunger, a thirst that was unquenchable and for relishing in the euphoric feeling that came when my blood roared with corruption.

"Have you any idea what you've done? What you have awoken? You haven't a clue how much I am fighting the need to hurt you right now!"

She blinked at me, her eyes locked on mine as she licked her lips. I narrowed my eyes when I felt her fingers play at the buckle on my belt. I didn't move, my fingers still wrapped around her elegant throat as she pulled my belt slowly, sliding it through each loop until she had the whole of it in her hands.

She lifted it, offering it to me. I frowned, confused at her action. "Then don't fight it," she whispered.

My breath hitched when the air in my lungs solidified. My eyelids felt heavy. My ears hummed as excitement coursed through me, every single hair on my body lifting as adrenaline vibrated through my core.

I relaxed my hold, sliding the palm of my hand slowly down her throat. "You want the pain, swan? You want to play?"

She didn't answer me but the way her eyes fired told me her response. Lowering my eyes to my hand, I moved it further down, lifting my other to join it. She gasped when I tugged on the neckline of her shirt and tore it down the middle. Her breasts were covered in a simple white bra, her dark nipples straining under the sheer material, her arousal hardening them. The simplicity of it was more arousing than the sexiest lingerie, its plainness as erotic as red lace.

Her mouth fell open when I ripped it in two at the front, her shock at my strength pleasing me. The plump flesh of her bare breasts hardened my cock further, her pert nipples dark and fat.

My legs nearly gave way and I had to palm the wall when she dropped to her knees before me. Her fingers slid the zip of my trousers, her eyes still secured on mine when she freed my erection from my underwear.

"You want me to suck you… Master?"

The familiar cold smile tugged my lips. I fisted her hair, pulling her head back slightly as I stared at her. "Do you realise what you're doing? What you are asking of me?"

She nodded in my strict hold. "Yes, I understand." She blinked slowly before her own cruel smile covered her face. "And yes, I want this. Although I'm sure that disappoints you."

I laughed coldly. "Not really. The pleasure I receive in the delivery of pain makes no difference if it's accepted or not."

She leaned forward and kissed the end of my cock, generating a deep hiss from me. "Then break free for a while. Allow yourself this. Deliver and thou shall receive."

I blinked at her odd words but shivered when her lips parted and she sank her mouth all the way down the length of me, her tongue pushing against the underside to sheath me tighter. My eyes secured on her mouth, her lips wrapped tight around my cock as she slid me in and out of her. She took the whole of me, loosening her throat to allow for the excess. She gagged slightly, her eyes watering. The torment her own actions brought upon herself boosted my lust making me strengthen my grasp on her hair.

Her eyes lifted back to mine when I started to control her movements, thrusting my hips as I pulled her deeper onto me, her eyes lighting with the dominance I directed her with.

She groaned and dropped the belt before her fingers curled around my testicles, her nails raking over the puckering of skin underneath. Sinking my teeth into my bottom lip as bliss enlivened something within me, I watched the ecstasy ghost across her face. She was relishing in my guide, allowing me to manage every single one of her moves. I couldn't explain the exhilaration that flowed through me. To make this usually confident and regulated woman lose all structure and succumb to my demand was invigorating, almost breath-taking.

Curling my fingers around her chin I directed her to stand. She stood, a little shorter than me, her eyes fixed on mine as though she awaited instructions. I bent, picking up the belt and curled it around my hand. I didn't miss the way her chest heaved and the way her nipples pebbled with her fierce arousal.

I tilted my head, studying her before I lifted the belt in front of her. "Do you understand what I am capable of?"

She gave me a simple nod. "Yes. You don't seem to understand what I'm capable of though." Her lips twisted into a mocking sneer. She slipped out from under me. I turned to watch her as she popped the button on her jeans and pushed them down her long legs. The paleness of her thighs once more demanded my gaze, the expanse of milky white skin quickening my heart beat. As though reading my thoughts, she turned, her bare arse now giving my eyes something to appreciate. Each buttock was firm, her vigorous regime evident in the taut skin and pert cheeks.

She glanced at me over her shoulder, her eyes on fire. "You see how pale my skin is, Daniel?" Her taunting was dangerous. My fingers manoeuvred the belt until the buckle was wrapped around my wrist, the leather strap now doubled and taut across the palm of my hand. Every fibre of me was alert and stimulated. It had been so long since I had delivered any extreme pain that my body was over-stimulated and a shiver racked my brain, excitement thinning my blood until it was powering around my body, the pulse of it throbbing in my ears.

The slow blink of her eyes captivated me, my mouth watering at the liberation of the old me. "Make me bleed," she ordered. "Make me scream... Master."

"Bend over the bed."

She was now naked, the whole of her stunning body open for my viewing. I had never seen a woman so fit, and it was beautiful. Each of her muscles gave her contours and lines that appealed, and although she was firm, she was still feminine. The curve of her breasts when she palmed the bed made my dick groan.

She still watched me as I stepped towards her. Her breathing was hard as she anticipated the pain, the freedom it could provide. Her lips parted when I softly ran the palm of my hand down the bend of her spine and then over her smooth backside. She was correct; her skin was pale, beautifully fair. The need in me to alter that into the deep glow of agony was engulfing.

She gasped when I lifted and brought my hand down hard, readying her for the leather. Her skin instantly flushed, the rush of blood to the surface thrilling every nerve within me. The next crack blushed more, her bottom lifting this time to meet me and grant her even more delicious pain.

She groaned when I gave her more and rested her forehead on the bed. Her skin glowed, not just from my hand, but the whole of her, the excitement racing though her forcing her blood to flow easier and more smoothly.

This was what the acceptance of pain offered. The endorphins that stimulated the brain released adrenaline, which in turn excited the heart, powering the blood to surge through the system, consequently stimulating every single erogenous zone in us.

"Harder," she moaned through her panting. "Don't be afraid to let me see you. Let yourself go."

I closed my eyes, trying to rein in the desire to hurt further but suddenly it was no good. She had roused the real me with her want for stimulation, with her acceptance.

The leather felt too good in my hand, its weight satisfying as though it was a part of me, my own personal tool. The whoosh it created when I whipped it through the air and down on her skin released the first of my own moans. Her body bowed under the contact, her mouth open to release her own erotic groan, her neck bent back as her face expressed the ecstasy.

The second slash broke her skin, releasing bubbles of her blood to pool over the paleness. I stared at it in awe, the beauty of the crimson against the white was mesmerising, stimulating. My groin throbbed, my own aroused blood hardening my erection severely.

Freedom overtook and I relished in each whip on her, every single crack driving the power in me higher and higher. I gave her what she wanted, what I needed, what I always craved. I slaughtered her body, destroying her skin, and finally broke her pain barrier when she screamed my name in a fierce climax. I watched her body stiffen, her head snap back further, her pale skin erupt in goosebumps and her lips part in an incredible orgasm. She was extraordinary as her body let go and allowed her to fly.

My balls clenched and I feared I would come right there watching the ecstasy take her.

Positioning myself behind her I murmured a groan when the trickle of her arousal dripped down the inside of her thighs. Fuck! I didn't wait for her to come down before I slammed inside her. Her climax gave me a graceful entrance, her slick walls allowing me all the way in on the first drive.

"Shit!" she hissed when I smashed against her cervix.

My palm crashed over her sore arse, igniting another hiss from her. "Watch your mouth. It's bad enough I have to listen to your filth, but I won't tolerate it whilst I'm inside you."

She stilled. I watched with a smile when her teeth sank into her lip, her anger at my declaration tightening her pussy around me, making my need to hurt her intensify.

"When my cock is pleasuring you, your body is mine, swan." Pulling out of her slowly, smirking at the way her hips followed me, I tore back into her hard, knocking her forwards up the bed. "Mine to control and mine to rule." Wrapping her hair around my hand, I tugged her backwards onto me, my cock feeding her pleasure. "I will give you what you want." I pulled her back against my chest and slid my fingers around the front of her throat. "So you will concede to mine."

She didn't reply, yet I saw the rage pour through her. My fingers constricted her airway further, her small gasps igniting the delight in pain deliverance inside me. After all her stubbornness and her defiance, I could still rule her. I was the one in power now, and better still, she knew it. She needed me, she craved what I could give her.

She was just like the rest, a puppet allowing me to manipulate them so long as they got what they wanted. However, it didn't disappoint me. Connie was somewhat different. I could see her discipline, the way she had been taught to devour pain was astounding. Her own manipulation of pain saddened me. She was like every woman I had educated but her schooling had been brutal, the scars that adorned her back testament to that.

I fucked her hard, knowing she could take it. My pelvis crashed against her sore backside over and over as both of our moans fuelled our hunger. Releasing her neck from my hold, I pushed her back down until she was flat on the bed, my body eclipsing hers, my whole frame pinning her down under me, her stitches scratching at my back, grazing my skin.

The position clamped her legs together, restricting my cock inside her but this only gave me a deeper sensation of her cunt biting down on me. The elegance in the way she fucked made my name for her even more appropriate.

I brought my mouth to her ear as I pushed further inside her, my thrusts quickening as my orgasm demanded its release. She groaned long and intensely when I swelled inside her, my climax painful and rapturous at the same time as I spewed inside her.

My teeth clenched and I growled loudly as my body clenched and jerked, bliss making my eyes roll and my heart beat stutter. She followed me, another orgasm ripping another scream from her, enhancing my own with the erotic sound.

I rested my forehead on her shoulder, sweat from both of us dripping down her hot skin, and slid out of her. She pushed up on her hands, encouraging me to roll off her and onto the bed.

Her face turned to me, her skin flushed and glowing. "Well fuck." My eyes widened at her language, especially after my earlier instruction but she winked. "I think you'll find your dick isn't currently inside me. So… yeah, fuck!"

She tapped my nose then lifted herself off the bed and walked into the bathroom.

My teeth were still grinding in fury as I heard the shower start up.

CHAPTER TWENTY-TWO

'Ghosts and Phantoms.'

Connie

THE EXHAUSTION DEBILITATED my weary body. I could take no more. I dropped to my knees again, wet mud adding a layer to the dry mud that caked my legs.

I no longer registered the pain, only numbness and an overwhelming need to die.

"Get up," Frederik hissed. I cried out, surprising even myself at the strength my body found to voice my anguish when he brought the whip across my back in punishment. I didn't howl at the agony, only the despair.

"I can't, Master," I managed to croak out, even though my body defied my words and I palmed the ground to push myself upright. My hand slid in the sludge and I fell forwards, my cheek gliding over the dirt, some of the earth slithering up one of my nostrils. The rain that beat down on me made my skin even heavier, making standing even more excruciating. Even the Gods hated

me apparently.

The slurry of dirt picked up by the leather of the whip fed my flesh when my skin split with yet another thrash from my Master. "Get up, Shadow!"

Swallowing slowly, I urged myself to stand, the tearing rain laughing at me when its strength mocked me and made the task almost impossible. I didn't care that my bare arse stuck up in the air, I didn't care that blood and mud were now my clothes, I didn't care that my beautiful long black hair had been hacked off, nor did I care that my skin hung off my protruding ribs. The only thing I cared about was my sister, and how my pain and agony gave her peace and happiness. And that in itself gave me the determination to stand once more.

Once upright, Frederik walked around me, coming to a halt in front of me. Rain poured from the umbrella Panther stood holding above his head and cascaded down my face but I knew better than to move from its torrent. I stood still, my eyes blinking furiously as the river lashed over my eyelashes and instinct attempted to close them. I didn't even have the energy to close my mouth as it hung open, the only available input and outpour for air now the mud blocked my nose.

He stepped forward, his foot skidding in the wet earth and his body surging forwards. Panther snatched his hand out and grabbed hold of him. I secretly wished he hadn't done that.

He curled his fingers around my throat and I sagged in his hold, thankful at the support for a brief moment. "What the fuck Isaac sees in you is beyond me. You are weak. A disabled irritant in an existence only for warriors and fighters." His hold on me tightened. I couldn't fight him anymore, I didn't have the energy. I wanted to die, I craved for it.

Frederik had taken an instant dislike to me as soon as Isaac had made me take my first step into the life of the Phantoms almost three years ago. As soon as I had entered the house, I felt his hatred seep into me. No Phantom ever went back on a binding contract, and the fact Isaac had brought me back instead of killing both Mae and me was not only outrageous but disrespectful to Frederik. So I was to be punished, not just for my father's debts, but for Isaac's insult.

I dropped to the ground when he opened his hand, screaming at the pain that erupted through my kneecaps when they smashed on the concrete. I knew I had shattered one, my malnutrition made them brittle and fragile. The agony made my body jerk and vomit spew from my belly. I was surprised there was anything to throw up. I hadn't eaten for days and I was concerned it was my stomach lining that had torn away when a spray of blood coated Frederik's legs.

He tutted, his cold stare locking on what painted him. My body instinctively curled in on itself when the heel of his boot slammed into my stomach. I had thought the pain before that had been unbearable but this was something altogether worse. Yet it wasn't the pain from his kick that ripped my soul from me, it was the fact that I knew his cruelness had just killed the tiny living person that was growing inside me.

A wail shattered the air around us when I immediately felt the warm rush between my legs, the torturous sound only a mother losing her child could make.

"What the hell?" Frederik barked when his eyes dropped to the rush of blood flowing over my thighs.

"No!" His scream was both agonising and welcoming. My eyes lifted in time to see Isaac race from the house and plunge the knife straight through Frederik's gut, his rage twisting it cruelly, his wrath dragging it back out so he could stab the bastard in the heart.

Frederik's body dropped beside me, his dead open eyes fixed on me. Blood trickled from the corner of his mouth and merged with my own.

"No!" Isaac wailed as he lifted me gently in his arms. Panther stood, his mouth agape, his eyes wide and flicking between Frederik and Isaac. "Contact the medic, have him meet me in the infirmary!" Isaac barked out as he rushed through the courtyard *with me. "Panther!"*

The world was leaving me, Heaven closing in, the angels tempting me with serenity as they welcomed my baby into their arms.

"Stay with me, my love. Don't you dare close those beautiful eyes," Isaac whispered as he ran. "Look at me, Connie." The fact that he used my name and not my tag made me slowly open my eyes. Minions only had tags. We lost our names the moment we walked through those large wooden doors.

His feet slipped in the wet mud but he kept going, his vigour and strength the only thing keeping me from death. "I'm going to fix you, that I will promise. I'm going to fix this." He lifted his hand to my face, his power and my frailty allowing him to carry me with one arm whilst he continued to move fluidly through the house. "I love you," he stated matter-of-factly. "I love you, Connie. We'll get through this. I promise."

I stared at him. Using what little energy I had left, I lifted my own hand slowly to his handsome face. I didn't have the ability to voice my own declaration but as I pressed my hand into his wet cheek, I managed a faint smile.

He sucked on his lips, his despair showing a side to him I had never seen. The death of our child not only gutted him, but gave him the strength to voice his emotions. Isaac didn't ever allow his feelings to control him, yet in that moment, he understood as did I that any hope I had ever had of having children had been snatched from me. And I would never be the same girl again.

Hardness overtook my heart. Detachment overruled my spirit. And grief tortured my soul.

I gasped for breath as I bolted upright. My heart was banging in my chest, sweat poured down my face, tears stung my eyes and my soul wept. Closing my eyes, I attempted to steady myself and claim back a regular rhythm in my pulse as I tried to stem the flow of tears. What the fuck?

Daniel murmured from his bed by the far wall. My head

spun, my eyes narrowing to study him in the darkness. He was still sleeping. I wasn't sure if I was grateful or sad.

Loneliness slithered through me until I shivered. "What the hell?" I whispered into the emptiness, hoping the sound of my own voice would block the grief pouring through me.

A strangled sob wrenched its way up my throat but I swallowed it back. I wouldn't allow it. *Couldn't* allow it. Its torrent would finish me.

Manoeuvring myself out of bed, I grabbed my phone from the table and shut myself in the bathroom.

"PIC Financial services," her tart voice greeted me.

"Four-three-two-nine. I require a call back from the management."

It was over five minutes before my phone buzzed in my hand and I swiped the connect icon immediately.

"Connie? Are you okay?" I swallowed at the overwhelming sense of homesickness that attacked me. "Connie?"

"I…"

A silent moment passed. "Talk to me. What's happened? Are you hurt?"

"No," I answered immediately to calm him. "No, I… I had the dream again." I squeezed my eyes closed, fighting the need to cry.

I sensed his frown, his confusion. "Again? Why, it's been years?"

"I don't know," I whispered. "I don't know why, Isaac."

He sighed. "My love, listen to me. I won't tolerate this again. I have never once regretted killing my father for you, for our child. He was a sick and evil dictator who deserved to die a thousand times over for what he did to you…. To us." His voice was stern knowing it was what I needed right then. "What's brought it on?"

"I don't know. I'm just feeling… a little lost," I admitted, cringing at the need in my voice. I hated that I was putting this on him.

"Do you need me to come to you? Or would you rather come

home and I'll arrange for a replacement to finish this contract?"

My eyes widened at his offer. It was never an option to decline or back out of a job, and for Isaac to be giving me that choice made me realise I was being weak and stupid.

"No," I replied with more sincerity than I felt. "I'm okay. I just needed to hear your voice."

He paused then tutted. "Are you missing my amazing cock? Is that what this is about?"

I couldn't hold in the chuckle as a smile lifted my lips and my spirit. "You have me all worked out."

"My love, I know you only married me for my sexual abilities, so it comes as no great shock to me."

"Well." I chuckled. "It isn't your finger I enjoy putting a ring on."

He laughed loudly and I grinned into the darkness. "Talking of toys, I have something special awaiting your return, so you need to get this job over with and then I can fill my face with your delicious pussy. My hunger is refusing to be sated with these flimsy things that insist on sharing my bed, I need a fight. Plus they're nowhere near as cuddly as you."

My jaw dropped. "Are you calling me fat?"

"My love, I would be the happiest man on the planet if you would gain a few pounds, you know that. You're too thin. My meat appreciates meat."

I giggled. "I'd rephrase that before Hunter thinks you're finally accepting what he's wanted to give you for so long."

"Pfft, the only thing that is granted access to my arse is your little finger, and that's pushing my limits."

Smiling, I closed my eyes. "I love you. Thank you."

I could feel his soft smile, the one that only I had access to. "And I love you. You shadow my heart," he whispered referring to the reason he'd given me the tag 'Shadow'. "Be safe and use your head."

"I will."

I slid back into bed and curled up. I couldn't help placing my hand over my stomach, my barren womb, and sighing. I'd lost so much in life but nothing hurt more than knowing I would never grow a life inside me again. Isaac had accepted me even with my inability to provide him with an heir to the family. But I never could. Although I loved Isaac and he grounded me, I could never let the hatred towards my father go.

His selfishness and greed had been the very reason both mine and Mae's lives had taken the route they had. His selfish need to take another man's wife, his greed for money, had been the very things that not only ended his life, but also his children's.

CHAPTER TWENTY-THREE

'You will be the death of me.'

Daniel

"WE WENT TO the zoo, Daddy."

Connie narrowed her eyes at her laptop screen as Annie jabbered in my ear.

"Oh, wow. What did you see? Did the lions eat Auntie Helen?"

Her giggle lifted my aching heart. I missed my baby so much the physical pain was becoming unbearable. She was my spirit and my soul. She was also the reason I had put my old self in the cupboard and locked the door on it, yet now she was so far away, I could feel the Master creeping back in, his sadistic and cruel ways delighted in the freedom the gap between my daughter and me brought.

"No, silly. But a camel spat at her."

I squeezed my eyes closed like that would hold back the laugh that raged up my throat. "Oh dear, that's terrible."

She was quiet for a moment before she gushed, "I miss you, Daddy. Can't you come and get me yet?"

I closed my eyes for a different reason this time and swallowed the lump that formed in my throat with the sound of her desperation. "Oh baby, I miss you too but I can't, not yet. Soon though, I promise." I hated lying to her but what the hell was I supposed to say, 'Daddy's not going to be alive long enough to do that, baby'? The pain that tore through me was immense and I had to sit down, blowing out a long breath to calm the frantic beat of my heart. She didn't deserve this, but then again, I didn't deserve her. I never had and I'd thanked God daily for her, yet that had never been enough. It was time to pay for my past, my sins. I understood that, but it didn't stop the debilitating pain that locked down my soul every time I thought about leaving her alone. Connie said she had arranged for her to be well cared for – a new family. That was good for Annie, but she should have been with me. She was going to lose both parents and no child should ever go through that. One was bad enough – I should know.

"But…" Annie choked out.

"Hey, aren't you enjoying it with Auntie Helen?" Her silence caused the hair on the back of my neck to stand on end. "Baby?"

"She's… okay."

Connie glanced at me, her brow furrowed when she caught my anguish. "Annie?"

"Yep," she said suddenly. A voice mumbled in the background. I pressed the phone to my ear to catch Helen's words but they were too quiet. "I have to go Daddy, Auntie Helen says I need my bath." Her little voice tightened the restriction in my chest.

"I love you to the moon, baby." Pressing two fingers to my lips, I kissed them and placed them on the phone, squeezing my eyes closed as though the force of my need would carry them over to her.

"I love you to the sun," she whispered. "And the stars and the world, and Mars, Daddy… and Mars… and….."

"Oh baby…" I blinked as my phone beeped, notifying me to

the terminated call.

Something wasn't right. I could feel it, in my bones, in my God damn heart.

Connie was watching me, her eyes inquisitive when I turned to her. "What is it?" Her own voice was almost as tight as mine. She knew as well as I did.

I shook my head, "I don't know but…"

A bang at the door caused me to jolt.

"Bathroom!" Connie barked as she pulled a gun from her bag and clicked off the safety. "Bathroom, Daniel!"

"For Christ's sake, Connie. I'm going to die anyway, what difference does it make who does it?" I was so fucking angry. With her for thinking I would hide out in the bathroom and let a woman deal with whoever was at the door. At me for putting my daughter in a place she hated. For Helen for taking her anger at me out on Annie. For the fucking Gods for taking her mother from her… from me.

Her body brushed past me as her words hissed out. "Because I am to be the one who will watch the blood drain from you, Daniel. No one else is entitled to that. That's why."

If a repeat knock hadn't reminded me someone was at the door, I would have ripped the fucking smirk off her damn face.

"Be careful, Connie," I hissed back as she approached the door. "I'm only abiding to whatever you're doing here because of Annie, but there is only so much I will tolerate before I break your fucking neck and hang you out of the window by your own hair!"

She chuckled. Fucking bitch. "Well that was creative."

I took an enraged step towards her but she ignored me. "Who is it?" she shouted through the door.

"It's the laundry man."

I frowned when a choked gasp erupted from her. She flung open the locks and stared at the man on the other side. He was tall, a little taller than me. His dirty blonde hair was mussed. His chin was covered in light blonde hair and his eyes were the most vibrant green I had ever seen.

His thin lips curled until each corner was nearly touching his ears. "Hello, my love."

A sob formed from Connie before she launched herself at him, her legs wrapping around his toned body as she buried her face in his.

My brow quirked when he slammed her against the wall and kissed her back just as roughly. *Okay.* His hand came up to her breast, squeezing her forcefully as his hips thrust against hers. *Okay.* His mouth moved slowly down her neck, his teeth nipping and marking her immediately. "Fuck, I missed you, Shadow. My cock is crying out for his perfect partner." *Okay.* Her fingers curled into his hair, pulling his face back to hers. They devoured each other. And I stood there and watched.

"What are you doing here?" she finally asked when they prised their lips off each other.

His brow creased before he sighed and lowered her back to the floor. "Unfortunately, I haven't just come to screw my beautiful wife into next week." *Ahh, okay.* "We need to talk."

She frowned at him, her head tilting slightly to the side. I sensed her apprehension, the hairs on my own body matched the ones stood to attention on her arms. "Isaac?"

His dark eyes found hers before they swung to me. He roamed them over me for a moment before turning back to Connie. "I think you better sit down."

"Isaac, just tell me." He quirked a brow at her stern tone but she rolled her eyes. "Please tell me what is wrong, my darling," she rectified with a sweet manner.

"Much better." He winked before his face dropped again and he sighed. "I need to know where you placed Annie."

Connie's back slammed straight. "Why?"

His fingers enveloped her jaw, pulling her face towards his. I shivered at the memory of my fingers holding her sister's in exactly the same pose. "Tell me, Connie."

"Isaac, this isn't in the rules. You give me the contract, I complete it. No questions are asked, no details are given."

He pulled in a deep breath. "You think I don't know that? I own you, Shadow. I own every single fucking Phantom. I made the rules to protect every single one of you."

I stepped forward when he pushed her back against the wall but stopped when she lifted a hand to me. "It's okay, Daniel."

Isaac turned his head slowly. A cold smirk tilted his lips and he chuckled. "Ahh, yes, I seem to have forgotten about your... mmm. I suggest if you don't want your guts decorating the wall, you stay exactly where you are."

"What the fuck?" I disregarded his warning and took another step into them.

"Daniel!" I narrowed my eyes on Connie as she spat a caution. "Honestly, it's okay."

Isaac stared at me, his expression mocking and goading. "Well?"

Flicking another glance at Connie she gave me a glare, again warning me. Going against everything my body was screaming at me, I lifted my hands. "Fine, but hurt her and I won't just stand here. You want to find out what I'm capable of, then go ahead."

They both gawped at me, Connie with her mouth wide open and Isaac with a confused stare. He started to chuckle, then full on laughed as he turned to Connie. "Well, my love, it looks like you've acquired an admirer." He leaned into her ear, whispering just loud enough for me to overhear. "Did you let him in your arse? He seems smitten."

"Fuck you."

He winked and dropped her throat, shaking his head as though disappointed with her. "There's only you I would do this for," he breathed as his fingers cupped her cheek lovingly, his mood shifting so quickly I was winded.

"Isaac, what?" I didn't miss the way she pushed her cheek into his touch, her eyes glazing with a softness.

"Trust me, Connie?"

She sighed, blowing out an irritated breath. "You know you're the only one I have ever trusted in my life. Isaac stop playing with me, I'm not a toy."

She gasped when he pushed against her, trapping her beneath himself and the wall. "You're – MY – fucking – toy!"

She licked her lips, her chest heaving. "Always," she whispered. What the fuck! They were the oddest couple I'd ever met, but there was something both of them displayed in their gazes and glares to each other that I had only ever seen once before - A look in my own eyes when I had watched the life drain from another.

"Who has Annie?" he repeated.

As though fighting with herself, Connie shivered. "She's with Daniel's sister."

Time seemed to pause for a single second. Isaac's body tightened, his lungs sucking the air from the room as he inhaled the deepest breath I had ever heard. He turned to me, his glare cold but one that wouldn't bear compromise. "Her name?"

I flicked a glance at Connie. I trusted her, but him, I wasn't so sure. She gave me a slight nod. "Helen Reynolds."

He stepped back and turned to Connie. "Did you vet her?"

She frowned at him, annoyance playing across her face. "Of course I did!"

He nodded slowly, his lips parted as his tongue trailed across his lip. "Not well enough, my love."

That single sentence had my knees buckling and every single nerve in my body crying out in pain. Goosebumps exploded over every inch of me as my stomach vaulted and vomit surged up my throat. My head shook from side to side before I even realised I was moving. "What? What does that mean?"

I pushed my hand into his chest, anger at his riddle bringing forward my wrath. Air gushed from my lungs. I blinked, my cheek squashed against the wall, a knife stuck across my throat in an instance. I wasn't even aware he had moved. Holy fuck! Now I understood the talk about the lead Phantom, and why he was in control of such a formidable *business*.

"You ever fucking touch me again and I will slice you into so many tiny little pieces that even the worms will be able to feast on you."

"Isaac!" Connie warned as she rushed over to us. "It's okay. It's his daughter. You would be the same."

He turned on her so quickly I was dizzy with each of his swift movements. "I never got the fucking chance though, did I? And you…" he spat. "You are still trying to fill that gap with someone else's child!" His hands covered her face before he'd even finished his vicious words. "I'm so sorry, my love. I shouldn't have said that."

Her face tightened as her lips disappeared behind her teeth but she nodded and placed her own hand gently on his cheek. "I know." It was whispered but the grief in her tone was so very loud.

"Will you stop fucking playing with each other and tell me what the hell is going on?" I didn't care if he gutted me right there in the hotel, I couldn't cope with what my mind envisioned.

He sighed, letting my anger ride over him. "A single contract was taken out on you, and then one including you and your daughter. Luckily for you, and unfortunately for the client, they are unaware of our refusal to hurt any child. The child is always placed with alternative carers with new names and new lives to protect them."

My estimation of the Phantoms rose tenfold with his declaration but I remained quiet and allowed him to continue.

"The dual contract was taken out by… Helen Reynolds."

I watched Connie drop to the floor as did I. My whole life rushed at me, snapshots of my beautiful Annie, all of them bombarding my mind one after the other in rapid succession, each one shattering my heart more and more.

"No!" Connie wailed. "No, Isaac."

He gripped her arms tightly and pulled her upright. Her head was shaking from side to side, her ashen face crumbling under the torrent of tears. "What have I done? What have I done?" she repeated over and over.

My eyes widened when Isaac shot his hand across her cheek, her skin flushing instantly. "Look at me!"

Her sobs were loud and almost as heart-breaking as the knowledge that my own sister wanted her only niece dead. "You are no longer a Swift. You are a Phantom. Rein it in." He pulled her further into him, his words hitting her with a fury. "I taught you better than this! Find the Phantom inside you. You need that fucker, you need to find the shadow that eclipses your heart and pull it free for what needs to be done."

I watched as her body went stiff. "Lock it down, Shadow," Isaac continued. "Do not mourn your sister. Avenge her. Fight for her. Honour her in the best way only you know how."

Her eyes closed for a brief moment before she opened them and nodded. "I'll need a safe house, an execution zone, Panther and Bullet."

Isaac smiled the cruellest of smiles. "There's my girl." He nodded once. "I'm on it. You have enough ammo?" She replied with a nod as she strode almost mechanically across the room.

"You really think she'll be in the place you left her?" I asked, knowing that Helen would have immediately taken Annie somewhere unknown.

"No," Connie answered in the coldest voice I had ever heard from her.

I couldn't hold in the choked sob that wrenched itself free from my throat but I watched over Connie's shoulder as she fired up the program she used to locate each of our microchips. A map loaded up. She hit numerous buttons on the keyboard and almost instantly a small pink dot blinked at us.

I stared at her. "You gave my daughter a microchip?"

She glared at me. "You really think I would do that?"

"Then how the hell do you have her blinking away on the screen?"

"That's not her. It's Herbert, her bunny."

I didn't know whether I wanted to kiss her or bend her over the desk and fuck the living daylights out of her in gratitude. As though reading my mind, she stood up, pulled out a leather wrap and unrolled it, displaying to me various knives as she winked.

"You can thank me later."

"Well, this I would love to see." Isaac chuckled from across the rooms as he leant against a wall and watched his wife with pride.

Glancing at Connie, determination and coldness surrounding her, I knew I was to witness something terrifying come to life, but she was equally astonishing when the Phantom inside her came out to play. I licked my lips, squirming at the way my cock strained against my shorts.

"Do you need me?" Isaac asked her.

She smiled softly. "Always. But I'll have to wait until this is done."

He nodded and pulled out his phone as he pulled the hotel door open. "I'll have everything prepared for you. Alert me to the rendezvous point for Panther and Bullet. Be safe and use your head, Shadow."

"I will." She gave him a glance that broke my heart for her. Their love was so very strong. I didn't acknowledge the loneliness that curled through me.

"I love you," she whispered across the room to him.

"Almost as much as I love you." He pulled the door closed behind him.

I watched her prepare her tools and weapons, staring in awe at the numerous firearms she had in her possession. She turned to me. "Ready?"

I gave her a nod as she narrowed her eyes then sighed and handed me a pistol. "Do you know how to shoot?" I quirked an eyebrow and she shrugged. "Then let's go take out this bitch and bring your daughter home."

A strength I never would have expected poured over me. I couldn't explain what I felt but I knew deep within me that this woman who planned my death would save my daughter from hers.

CHAPTER TWENTY-FOUR

'Respect is earned not given.'

Connie

THE SILENCE IN the car was suffocating. Daniel had been staring out of the window, his mind elsewhere, or rather on Annie, the same as mine.

The rain bounced off the window, the wipers struggling to keep up with the river rippling across the windscreen. The wind had picked up, forcing the rain harder, the driving beat of it and the wipers regular rhythmic sway hypnotising in the quiet. I fought with the steering wheel as each gust blew the car across the empty motorway.

I glanced at him, not risking taking my eyes off the road for too long. "I need to know, Daniel." He turned to me. His face was so full of anguish that I moved my eyes back to the front before I spoke again. "I need to know what to expect. Why she's doing this."

I saw him nod slowly before he reached forward and adjusted

the heating after a small shiver shook his body. "Helen and I, we were close. She…"

I rolled my eyes and gritted my teeth when my phone rang. Glancing at the console, I hit the accept icon. "It's me," Bullet's tiny voice came from the speakers. "We're both prepped," she continued without waiting for me to speak. "We're awaiting your instruction."

"I'll send detail via secure connection. Although with the way the weather has deteriorated, I'm going to have to abort until morning."

Daniel's head snapped round to mine. Just as he opened his mouth I held up a hand, halting him.

"I agree," Bullet said. "We're around ten miles from the centre. We'll settle and await your correspondence."

"Okay."

"The other requirements you needed are set. And…" She sighed and I frowned. Bullet was never one to mince her words yet I could sense her struggle. "And you know that I will do anything to…" She clicked her tongue, knowing that we weren't on an encrypted network and had to be careful how she worded things. "What is needed. Anything… *Anything.*"

"Family is more than blood," I whispered back to the closest person I had ever had as a friend. I knew she would understand my words after she had just told me she would sacrifice herself for my niece and me.

"And blood is what makes us family," she replied giving me cause to smile. "We bleed together, my friend." Her parting words calmed my anguish.

"They are your family now." Daniel spoke into the darkness that had descended in the car.

I glimpsed at him and smiled. "Yes. Yes they are."

He nodded and gave me a very rare smile. "That's good, that you have them."

We were quiet for a moment. The road started to blur and I was finding it increasingly difficult to carry on driving. "We're going to have to stop."

"But we need to find her."

"Daniel." I sighed, trying to convey the truth in what I was to say. "For one, I can't do my job properly in a storm. I need it to be clear to grant me an opening to gain access and to survey the area properly. I can't risk anything for Annie. And Helen wants to hurt *you*. She is expecting us to find her. That's why she has taken Annie to your childhood home. She is waiting for you."

He rubbed at his face. "I know." He laughed bitterly and shook his head. "You know. I always expected some sort of avengement to be sought after the way my life has taken its toll on others, but to be perfectly honest, I always thought it would be one of the stock, or maybe the parents of a girl, even their husbands or investigators that have been hired by the family who would be the ones to finally grant me redemption."

I sighed and shook my head. "You think death is penance for your sins, Daniel?"

He turned to me, the faint light only showing me half of his bewildered expression. "Yes. Do you not?"

"No. Redemption is having each family member taken from you. It is giving your life for your sister's only to find that God had been cruel anyway, mocked you and your search for salvation. It is spending hours tied to a wooden cross in the bitter elements of winter, naked, bleeding and bruised while the rats start to feast on you. It is watching someone you love being raped and beaten just because you love them. It is having your soul ripped from you when the only child you were ever to conceive is killed so fucking brutally. It is hearing the cry of someone you love so desperately tear you apart."

He was silent, his face dropping to the floor as the forbidden words slipped from me. Why did this fucking man break every damn rule in me, tear down the walls I had erected around myself and pull truths out of me that had been buried long ago?

"And what exactly do you need to seek punishment for, swan?" I could feel his eyes boring through me, his stare penetrating my soul as he waited for my answer.

A sign for motorway services lit up on the left and I indicated, turning onto the slip road.

"We'll stay here tonight. It's too dangerous to carry on." I said, ignoring his question. Luckily he didn't push, just nodded as we pulled up to the small hotel. Sleep seemed so appealing right then. And I knew we'd both need it for what was to come.

"It was my fault," Bullet lied as Frederik held us both before him, Gregory holding me flat to the floor as Jacob pinned Bullet down by her hair.

"What?" I gasped. "No, no, Bullet."

"It was me, Master. I stole it!"

"Bull...." I cried out when Frederik's boot slammed into the side of my hip, the crack loud on contact. I wedged my lips together to stop the scream that wanted to hurtle from my throat.

"Refrain from talking. You are both liars. Liars and whores. I'm holding you both accountable."

Bullet's eyes shot to mine. "I'm sorry," she mouthed. I shook my head at her. I knew why she had done it, I even understood her. I would have taken the blame for her if she was pregnant, knowing what cruel torture Frederik would have lined up for us.

We both flinched when we were pulled up together, both of Frederik's puppets knowing what he wanted without him having to even voice a command. That's how manipulated we all were.

He walked slowly over to Bullet, his cold eyes making me shiver. He stood before her, looking over her as though she were an insect that had crawled over his food. I hated him so much. I wanted him dead. I wanted to kill him myself, and I think if it weren't for the fact he was my lover's father, I would have ended him by now. I had no doubt in my head I was capable. As Isaac had told me often enough, I was the most formidable Phantom of the whole clan. I also knew this was the only reason Frederik kept me alive, because I was useful to the family, not because of any compassion towards me. If he ever found out about my relationship with his son and heir, then I knew that would change with a snap of his fingers.

I flung forward when Frederik slammed his fist into Bullet's face, knocking her to the ground. Jacob and Gregory grabbed each of my arms, holding me back.

"Master, please don't."

He laughed, shaking his head. "You will see what your disobedience brings, Shadow. You refuse to be controlled. So maybe making your friends take your punishment may start to control you better." He turned back to Bullet. "You stole from me, so I think the only appropriate punishment is to steal something from you."

My eyes remained dry, my ability to cry stripped from me years ago, as my friend took my punishment. They raped her, each of them, after they broke her frail body. One after the other they took her and then all three of them together. Bullet never shed a tear. We held each other's eyes through the duration of both our visits to hell. Another piece of my soul shattered as her blood trailed along the ground and pooled against my foot where they had tied me to the pole that was fixed to the floor for occasions of punishment.

Their sick grunts twisted my stomach as Bullet's silence shredded my heart. It was then that I felt my baby kick for the first time. A moment of absolute joy held me up in that moment of sheer desolation. I couldn't close my eyes, I was made to watch what my actions for stealing some bread from the kitchens to feed my child had brought. We were all so very hungry, each one of us malnourished and weak. It was only because of this that I had managed to hide my pregnancy and I had been amazed at how my baby had *even survived in the devastating condition my body was in, hence the need to steal food. Unfortunately this time we had been caught as Bullet had kept watch for me.*

It was only when a solitary tear leaked from my best friend's eye and trickled across her cheek that the vomit came. "I'm so sorry, Bullet," I whispered. "I'm so, so sorry."

"Connie!"

"I'm so sorry. I'm so sorry. I'm…"

"Connie!"

I jolted upright, my heart hammering in my chest, my lips tingling from the sweat dripping down my face. Placing my hands over my face I urged myself to wake.

"You were dreaming," Daniel said. He pushed my hair from my cheeks, concern on his face. "Are you okay?"

I nodded, unable to form words as my body trembled. Slipping from the bed I walked into the bathroom and flicked on the shower, eager to wash away the sweat, and the nightmare.

The visions continued to assault me as I sat on the toilet, emptying my bladder but using it as support against the tremble in my legs.

"I love you, Shadow. I'd take anything for you," Bullet whispered as I dabbed at her wounds with the damp cloth. "I'd die for you."

"Connie?" Daniel's voice snapped me out of my memories.

"What?"

He stared at me. "I said I'll run you a bath instead." My brow lifted when the turn of him displayed the tattoo adorning his right shoulder. A stunning blue butterfly seemed to ripple over the contours of his strong shoulders, its wings spread and almost flickering with each of his movements. The unique colour matched the reflection in my eyes, in Mae's eyes. My eyes dropped to read the script below.

*'The blue of your eye
is the beauty in the butterfly.
It's time to spread your wings
and soar up high.
Your soul is now eternally free,
and in my heart forever you will be.'*

Words stuck in my throat. Pain rippled through my core but a deep feeling of something softer burrowed inside, bringing a soft smile to my lips. His love for Mae astounded me. I couldn't hold back the feeling that she had managed to procure love before she had left. Before witnessing the tattoo, I'd struggled over whether Daniel's love had been enough for her, but now, now the pain eased it was so very obvious Daniel had loved my sister with an engulfing force. And she deserved that.

I watched him take a complimentary sachet of bath oil and pour it under the running water. "It will help relax you."

"Okay. Where's the Master and what have you done with him?"

I blinked in surprise when he turned to me, his fingers choking my throat. Whoa! A smile turned my lips when I noticed the heave of his chest, and the strain in the shorts he had been sleeping in. "There he is," I croaked out.

He lifted me effortlessly, the hold on my neck secure. I could have easily taken him, but I was enjoying the darkness that had descended. He was like Jekyll and Hyde, his mood swings frequent and sharp. I liked this side of him, it was sexy, and it turned me on to see the depravation that lived inside him.

Call me sick and twisted but after being *adapted* to enjoy pain, there was no greater pleasure than being fucked so hard and brutally that you could feel the flow of blood race around your body, adrenaline and lust driving your heart beat higher and higher as pleasure and pain poured into every nerve of your stimulated body.

He glared at me, his eyes burning a hole through me. "I buried him years ago. I don't need him to love my daughter. I don't need him to see the rise of the fucking sun every morning. And I don't need him to live any more. Annie is my life, not the past. The future."

I nodded as much as I could. "I understand." And I did, totally. He eyed me warily when I smiled. "But maybe once in a while, when the need for a dirty fuck arises, you should let him free."

His chest heaved with my words, his stare growing colder. "What the fuck is wrong with you?" I didn't know whether to slap some sense into the bastard or laugh at him. "You continually push all the wrong buttons, Connie. Why? Why do you encourage me to set him free?"

His fingers loosened on my neck. I tilted my head and considered him for a moment. "You know, I think in that head of yours, you struggle to differentiate between sentiment and need. Sex and love. Life, as you say, should be lived for those around you, to consider Annie's place in your life and adapt to her must have taken great sacrifice, and I applaud you for that. But Annie isn't your life, Daniel. She is your heart, your family. You need to carry on living." I held my hand up when he opened his mouth. "And yes, you say Annie gives you life, but she can never take away your past, or who you truly are."

He continued to stare at me, his mouth open in shock at my words. I chuckled. "I'm not saying you should go out, kidnap a girl and torture her. But what I'm trying to say is, that it's okay to be yourself now and again, as long as no one is hurt and all parties are on board."

His face softened as he considered my words. "Daniel." He blinked at me, swallowing hard. "You will kill yourself if you lock everything down. It will suffocate you. Annie needs you happy, or she will never be."

His face paled slightly as he dropped his arm completely. The room seemed to sway beneath me with his next words.

"I loved her so very much," he whispered into the silent bathroom, his sad eyes locked onto mine. "She found me, Connie." I gulped at the despair suddenly clogging the air around us. "She found the real me, and she dragged it out of me whether I wanted her to or not."

"And now you're frightened if you push aside the real you for the Master that you'll never be able to find him again?"

His slow nod made me reach out and cup the side of his face. "Do you not think that Mae fell in love with both of you, the gentle and the selfish?"

"I'm not even sure she loved me," he confessed as he pushed his face in to my touch.

I smiled at him. "If she told you she did, then she did. She was the most honest person I know. Mae never spoke a lie just to make someone feel good about themselves, even if it got her into trouble."

His smile grew into a grin. "I can vouch for that."

I smiled back and tilted my head to the bath. "It's full."

He frowned then realised what I meant and jumped back, turning off the taps. "In."

I shrugged and pulled my t-shirt and knickers off, smirking to myself at his amazement. His eyes wandered hungrily as I slid down, the comforting warm water easing the tension in my muscles.

"Oh God, that's good." He nodded and turned to leave. "Join me?"

He paused before sliding his shorts down his legs. His hard cock sprung free and he laughed when I licked my lips. "Hungry?"

"Oh, very."

He didn't waste time. He climbed in, one foot either side of me as he stood above me. His lips curled when he fisted his erection and started to slowly slide his hand up and down. "Get on your knees, Connie."

I nearly fist pumped the air at the tell-tale sign of the Master. "You want me to suck your cock?"

I gasped when his hand snatched my hair and he pulled me up onto my knees, the bath water sloshing over the rim with the sudden movement. "When I give you an order, you will obey it immediately. I won't tolerate hesitancy. And you will make sure to address me as Master."

I nodded, "I'm sorry, Master." God, how I loved to play.

"Do it again and I'm not sure you will appreciate the punishment." He quirked an eye humorously. "Although, I'm pretty sure you will."

I looked up at him with a small smile. His fingers spread across my jaw, prising my mouth open. His hold on my hair held me still when he slid his cock into my mouth. I couldn't close my mouth with his stern hold and I so desperately wanted to caress his cock with my tongue, cover him in the warmth of my mouth. He smirked when saliva dribbled out of the corner of my mouth and my throat clamped down to try and catch it.

"You will not suck on me until I tell you that you can. You need to earn the taste of me and I'm not so sure that you have."

I remained silent as he slipped further towards the back of my mouth, causing me to gag when he hit my tonsils. Wetness coated my mouth even more, my own spit now seeping onto my chin. He pulled out and ran the crown of his cock over my face, wiping my own fluid around.

"You want me to fuck your dirty little mouth, Connie? Do you want me to slide my cock between the press of your lips so you can wrap that vehement tongue of yours around me?" I nodded, keeping my eyes fixed on his. "Then ask me nicely."

He smiled when I didn't hesitate. "Please may I suck on your cock, Master?"

He leaned down, bringing his face to mine. His fingers dropped from my hair and wrapped around my throat. "Stand up and bend over."

I blinked in surprise but did as he asked, my body shivering at the lack of heat from the water. My bottom stuck up as I grabbed hold of the taps. His hands slid down my arms until he covered my hands with his. "Oooh," I murmured when he wrapped my own knickers around my wrists and secured my hands to the taps. They would snap easily if I needed a quick release so I wasn't concerned.

My eyes widened when he stuffed his boxer shorts into my mouth. "I won't tolerate the disgusting language you spill whilst I'm inside you, so this way, we can both enjoy fucking without upsetting one another."

I wanted to laugh but thought he wouldn't appreciate it, so I nodded, confirming I was okay with it. I squirmed when his mouth ventured down my back, his teeth nipping at my stiches and firing arousal into me as he slid one finger inside me.

"So wet already, swan. Your cunt drools for me, for the fill of my cock."

I pushed against him, curling my hips to pull his finger deeper. He stroked over my G-spot, flooding my pussy further and dragging a muffled moan from me. He withdrew and trailed my arousal up to my arse. I shivered and closed my eyes as pleasure spun into me when he worked his finger in.

"Oh, you like to be fucked in your arse?"

I nodded again, swallowing the eruption of saliva in my throat. My body was too sensitive as he started to fuck my backside with two fingers, spreading them wide to open me up in prep for him. Excitement caused goosebumps to erupt when I started to rock back on him.

I groaned when his lips enclosed over my swollen clit and he sucked hard. My hips bucked, bringing his fingers deeper inside me. His tongue pleasured me as his fingers forced my lust into a new level. I was grinding against him, begging him to provide me with the oblivion of climax. He was relentless, his mouth sucking, his tongue flicking, his fingers pumping so I soon cried out against the cloth in my mouth as bliss bolted me down, the pleasure constricting every single muscle in my body.

I giggled when he slammed his cock into my pussy, forcing me forward and prying the tap with the action. Cold water gushed from the spout as he started to ram into me harder and harder, his rhythm unforgiving and brutal. My breasts swung with the movement, the water tickling my nipples every time he forced me forwards.

I managed to turn it back off when he pulled out of me and moved up to my anus, the tip of him easing in slowly as my muscles forbid him. I pushed back against him, opening myself for him. He groaned when he slid all the way in, his balls laid against my pussy.

He stared to move slowly, widening me, filling me, pleasuring me as his balls tickled my engorged clit, pleasing the stimulated flesh. He pulled out his underwear from my mouth and my tongue stuck to the material, making us both chuckle.

"I want to hear you," he grunted as he sped up.

I mumbled something incomprehensible but the long groan that forced its way out caused Daniel's cock to swell inside of me.

"Fuck!" he hissed when he pushed back in and out. I wanted to mock him, chastise him for his own use of language but I couldn't think straight, never mind voice words.

His fingers clawed at my hair as his other hand enclosed my neck, his hold tight and restrictive. My climax burst free instantly as the pain in my scalp poured excitement into my bloodstream and down to my pussy.

His drives into my arse were brutal but so very good. The friction of him dragged my climax into new heights, suspending my pleasure until I thought I would pass out from ecstasy.

"Your arse is milking me, Connie."

I gasped when he released my hair, grabbed my small bottle of shampoo and pushed it into my pussy. My back arched as my body cried out at the extra fill. "Oh fuck yes!" Daniel hissed as he slammed into me over and over, his hand working the bottle in and out of me simultaneously so both my arse and my pussy accommodated the stretch at the same time.

I was struggling to breathe as my lungs tightened with the pleasure taking over everything. My body vibrated with the need for release once again. There was only ever Isaac who had given me this much pleasure. Most of my partners had been greedy in their own needs, but I knew Daniel was forcing the pleasure into me for both our sakes, not just his own.

And that knowledge tipped me over the edge. I screamed as my body struggled to cope with the overload of chaos stimulating me.

I turned my face to the mirror just in time to see Daniel pull out of me and pump his cum all over my back. Floods of white creamy fluid shot from him. His body tensed and his teeth clamped together as he watched himself release dominantly over me.

His chest heaved as much as mine as we fought to breathe.

"Holy…" I smirked as Daniel snapped his eyes to mine in the mirror waiting for the torrent of filth I was about to voice. "Oh my," I joked, with a wide cheeky grin. "Goodness me, Master. You sure know how to make a lady feel good."

His lips twitched at my humour and he shook his head. He sat down in the water and reached round me to turn on the hot tap. "Sit down and let me clean you."

I pursed my lips at the offer but shrugged and did as he told me, squeezing my backside between his thighs. I leaned back against him and let my eyes close as he worked soap over me and gently washed me.

I didn't like the feeling it brought, but I sighed and shut down the emotion. Sex was sex, it didn't involve sentiment.

Up until now.

CHAPTER TWENTY-FIVE

'The breaking point comes at the most intimate moment.'

Daniel

SHE MURMURED HER appreciation when my fingers dug into her scalp. My eyebrow quirked when it actually sunk in that I was washing her hair for her. Annie filtered into my mind, how I would wash her hair, her mouth rampant as I massaged the cherry foam around her head.

"You're good at this." Connie sighed.

Leaning over the edge of the bath for the glass from the sink, I proceeded to rinse the suds from her, pulling her long brown hair. "You dyed your hair."

She chuckled and settled her back against my front, her stitches scratching my skin. "You are such a typical man."

"Typical? Is there any such thing?"

She chuckled and nodded. "Oh yeah. My hair has been brown

for days."

"Why?"

She turned her face to look at me over her shoulder. "Because I have work to do." She didn't offer any further explanation and I didn't ask for one. I would never understand women, but thinking about it, I rather liked the air of mystery around them. It had always appealed to me why they made the decisions they did. Their hearts and heads were always so conflicting, their heads usually correct most of the time, yet time after time, they chose to let their hearts rule them, even when it was blatantly obvious that they would get hurt.

"Your relationship with your husband is somewhat... unusual." I didn't know why I suddenly voiced my thoughts but Connie snorted.

"Yeah."

"Does he sleep with other women?"

She peered over her shoulder and smirked. "Isaac doesn't sleep with women, he fucks them. We only ever sleep with each other."

"But doesn't that... I dunno, hurt?"

She shook her head. "No. Fucking isn't personal, it's just getting pleasure from someone, using their body. The heart has nothing to do with sex. We don't have the most conventional marriages but I know Isaac loves me and would die for me."

"But sometimes sex is intimate. Aren't you concerned that he may find affection with one of his lovers?"

"No. Isaac is... he's very cold. You remind me of him a little. His childhood was hard, harder than mine and yours put together and to be honest, I'm not the most *romantic* girl." She chuckled. "He understands that I have needs and he sees to them, I also understand that he likes to fuck anything with tits so we just... work."

"Don't you ever get jealous?"

She tilted her head and sucked on her teeth. "Only once... oh, sorry, twice." She stiffened and I sensed her unease.

"What?"

"I found him bathing someone."

My eyes widened and roamed over us both, sat in the warm foamy water. "Oh?"

She hesitated. "We never do intimacy, as you call it, with others. But bathing, kissing, is considered intimate and that pushed all the wrong buttons for me when I found him with the skank."

"The skank?"

She shook her head. "It doesn't matter, that's a story for another day." I knew she was done, and I was amazed at how much she had disclosed.

I frowned when she took hold of my foot that was wrapped around her calf and pulled it up to her lap. Her earlier words of bathing being intimate confused me when she was completely contradicting herself with her touch but I refrained from judging her out loud. "Mmm," I mumbled when she lathered her hands then started to wash and massage my foot, her fingers gentle but her thumbs digging into the underside, the pressure on my sole relaxing as her fingers rubbed between each toe.

Picking up the sponge, I dipped it into the water and squeezed it over her chest, watching the rivulets stand above her skin with the oil in the water and trickle over her breasts, the journey over her dark nipples mesmerising as they pebbled with the contact.

She continued to massage me as I bathed her in silence, both of us valuing the calm before the storm.

She replaced my foot into the water and grabbed the other to start the same worship. My head dropped back against the rim of the bath and I sighed. "I haven't been this relaxed in years."

I felt her nod her head against me. She was quiet and I opened one eye to peek at her. "What are you thinking?"

She didn't answer for a while, her mind elsewhere as she ran the whole of her hand over my foot, her eyes watching as she spread the white lather over my skin.

"Were you with her?" Her quiet voice banged loudly on the ice that had formed around my soul. She felt me stiffen but she didn't apologise for her question.

"Yes." My own voice was quiet as hers had been but the ear-splitting roar of my heart beat was deafening. "Yes," I repeated with a whisper.

She nodded slightly. "Was she in pain?"

"No."

She paused then lowered my foot back into the water. "No?" I shook my head, knowing she would feel it. "But…"

"I helped her." I closed my eyes, praying for her to understand. "Have you ever danced with the devil, Connie?"

She scoffed and inhaled heavily. "Many times."

I nodded, not doubting it for a second. "I would dance with him again and again to make sure Mae went without a murmur of pain. I need you to understand that I know I'm not a good man, in fact I'm so far from good I know I will never meet Mae again, not in the next life anyway. But even if I had been a fucking angel, I will never regret… never regret killing your sister. I would sacrifice the promise of absolution to give her peace."

She took my hand and ran her fingers over mine, her touch faint and slow. "Thank you."

I blinked at her gratitude. I hadn't expected it, I had been anticipating her wrath but I smiled at her understanding. "She deserved so much more from life. But you know, she never once gave up. She fought with so much spirit that I was in awe of her. Even in the darkest times, her smile lit me up. I was so cruel yet she still smiled, she still reached out and touched me. She still looked at me and saw something that no one, not even myself, had seen." I sighed. "I don't know, they say the closer to death you are, the more you see. Maybe she saw what was to come for me after this life and her pity gave her the need to comfort. Whatever it was, I will never understand how she found me beneath all the aggression."

I watched her as she slipped around in the water to face me. A tear slid down her cheek and dropped off her chin onto her breast. Her sad eyes held me as she straddled my thighs and placed her palms over my cheeks. We remained still, looking at each other, saying so many things without words.

I shivered when she leaned forward and placed her mouth so gently over mine. Her lips were warm and soft, her tears tasting of salt on my tongue when she sobbed into me. I slid my hands around her back, holding her to me, giving her support as I kissed her back. Her gaze bore into me as her fingers journeyed up my face until she sank them into my hair and lowered herself onto my erection, her body tensing as I sank deeper inside her, the tight grip of her arching my back in pleasure.

Her lips parted as she moaned into me. I caught her bottom lip between my teeth, gently seizing hold of her as she started to move on me, her breasts squashed against my chest, her thighs clamped against mine and her pelvis rubbing tightly against mine.

She rocked on me so slowly the water didn't even ripple. Her hot breaths into my mouth brought on my own soft groans, her piercing blue eyes talking to me as she moved above me.

I pushed my hands through her wet hair, cupping the back of her head to pull her against me. I kissed her then, kissed her until we couldn't breathe, our eyes still locked on one another's. I kissed her until her sobs subsided and her heavy breaths began to be vocal. I kissed her until she pressed down hard against me and came with a short, sharp gasp, her body trembling over mine as I spewed my own release into her.

Her choked sobs caused my chest to throb as she dropped her forehead to my shoulder and cried. She cried for Mae, she cried for her. She sobbed for what her life was, and maybe even what mine was. She wept for her past and what the future held. But I held her to me and took it from her. I soaked it up, dragging her desolation from her as she clung to me and allowed me to see the real Connie; not the Phantom, not the assassin, not even Mae's sister, but Connie Swift, the lost girl who had been buried under all the hatred and regret.

CHAPTER
TWENTY-SIX

'Old enemies, new family, and the taste of blood.'

Connie

HER SMILE WHEN I parked the car beside the van in the old abandoned picnic site half a mile from Daniel's old home lifted my spirits. "Fuck, I missed you." I laughed when she grumbled at me as I hugged her and spun her round.

"Likewise, my friend," she whispered into my ear as I placed her feet back on the ground. Bullet was tiny. At four foot, eleven she was the smallest of the Phantoms, but her amazing shooting skills made up for her lack of physical power, although her ninja skills helped her along when she didn't have her gun with her.

"Panther, get your arse over here." I watched him roll his eyes in the back of the van before he smiled and jumped down, walking over to me and enveloping me in his strong hold.

"Looking good, girl." He winked as he held me at arm's

length and studied me. Since the day he had witnessed my baby leave my body, Panther had taken on the role as big brother in my life. I knew he would protect me and Annie with his life, and my respect for his compassion as well as his ability to attack swiftly and stealthily, hence his name, had been the reason we had worked together ever since. "It's been too long," he said as he gestured for me to follow him into the back of the van. He turned to Daniel and narrowed his eyes. Panther was very protective and I could taste his hatred for Daniel. "I'm surprised you've kept him around as long as you have."

I warned him off with a glare. He shrugged his shoulders and sighed before he curled his lip at Daniel. "You better come see this too."

Daniel frowned then climbed into the van with us, his eyes widening at the equipment kitting out what appeared to be a normal van on the outside.

I frowned when Panther tapped one of the four screens, each displaying various angles in and around the house.

"Who is it?" I asked, bending towards the screen to study the extra body showing. Panther and Bullet had arrived early and set up the equipment that gave us an insight to people in and around the house. The technology we had acquired from the Chinese, for a hefty price, had been worth every damn penny.

"I'm not sure," he said as he tapped his fingers on the keyboard, zooming the camera in further. It only allowed us to see silhouettes not actual images, more like thermal imaging but instead of red blurry figures in a vast of blackness, we saw everything from the layout of the house, the furniture around the house, to the outline of people and more importantly, weapons.

A small figure, definitely Annie, sat on the floor in the lounge playing with what I presumed to be two dolls. Helen was stood talking to a tall man in the kitchen. There were four more men outside, patrolling the grounds, as well as three more positioned around the house.

"Can you take the external ones?" I asked Bullet as I turned to her.

"Yep, no problem," she confirmed as she started to check and load her rifle.

"I gather you want the two main ones, so I'll take the interior guards," Panther said as he pulled various knives from a briefcase and sited them in different places about him.

"Okay." I nodded to them both as we each plugged our earpieces in, adjusting the tiny mic in front of our mouths and confirmed the plan.

"And me?" Daniel asked.

I frowned and turned to him. "You?"

"Where do you want me?"

"Here," I ordered.

He narrowed his eyes and stared at me with incredulity. "What? No, I'm in there with you."

"Uh-uh. You stay here. I will bring Annie to you."

"No, I'm coming with you."

Bullet and Panther eyed us then climbed from the van, giving us a moment when they sensed my anger.

"You will do as I say," I spat. "You will stay here and wait. This is Annie I'm going in for, not some random target I have no regards for."

"Yes! This is my daughter, and if you think I am going to sit back and put her life in yours and their hands then think again."

I pulled in a fortifying breath and rolled my head around my shoulders, recoating my dry teeth with my tongue. He groaned when I swiftly straddled him where he sat in a chair, my feet wrapping around his ankles and securing his feet as my thighs pinned his arms by his side.

I pressed the heel of my hand into the dip of his throat, instantly restricting his air supply. "If you think I am allowing you to go in there and snatch Annie from under me whilst my friends and I do the dirty job, then *you* can think again." He gasped and struggled beneath me but even with his strength he was no match for my fury. "I will *not* allow them to kill you, Daniel." His eyes showed his confusion but I smiled coldly. "I told you at the beginning, your heart beat is mine. I will be the one to witness its final throb. I will be the one that will force your soul into hell, no one else." I leaned further into him. "A Phantom never goes back on a contract. If you think the sex between us changes anything then you are mistaken. You are my original target, and you will be my final one."

He blinked and coughed when I released him. "Your final one?"

I considered him for a moment before I moved off him and picked up the weapons Panther and Bullet had brought for me.

"After you, I'm retiring."

"Why?" He eyed me sceptically.

"Because I have another job to do." I turned my back on him and jumped out of the van. "I'll be bringing up your daughter after your death."

I dropped down over the metal fence, making sure to land on the balls of my feet for a more silent approach. I never took my eyes off him as I crouched and moved along the perimeter. Just as I was about to pull my knife out he dropped down to the ground, his body hitting with a heavy thud. I chuckled when his friend on the opposite corner did the same.

"Bloody hell, Bullet." I laughed quietly into my mic. "Gimme a chance."

"Well, look who's late for the party," she retorted humorously. "First come, first served, loser."

"Well I had to fix my lippy first, you know how it goes for us pretty ones."

"Fuck you! Why do you think Isaac named you Shadow? It wasn't because you shadow his heart as he so sickeningly keeps saying, it's because you belong in the shadows, my friend, with all the ugly nutters. Of course you had to slap more slap on. After all, your doe-eyed boyfriend wants you at your hottest."

"What the fuck?" I moved further around the house, my eyes alert and sharp as I pushed my glasses up my nose. I hated wearing the things but I couldn't see further than ten metres without them. Panther had smirked at me when I curled my lip at them before grumbling something profane under my breath.

"Oh, don't what the fuck me," she said as I moved into position at the back of the house, my eyes flicking to every dark corner. "I saw the way he looked at you. He's smitten."

"Bullet. He is not smitten. We fucked, that's it."

"Uh-uh. You are going to break his heart." I rolled my eyes at her humour but couldn't help the lift of a smile when she started to sing Queen's *Another One Bites The Dust* in my ear.

"Will you two girlies shut the fuck up!" Panther barked at us, his loud growl in my ear deafening.

Bullet started laughing. "Aww, Panth, has Shadow stolen your man lollipop?"

My eyes widened as Panther huffed. "Go suck Shadow's pussy, Bullet. We all know you have the hots for her. After all, there has to be a reason you don't bang any men at the Phantom parties."

I tensed, sucking on my lips at the banter that had turned into something personal. "Come on, guys. Let's play nice." I cringed when only Panther acknowledged me. "Bullet?"

"Bullet?" Panther blasted my earpiece when silence greeted us. "Bullet!"

"I'm here," she replied. "Sorry, mic's playing up."

My heart hurt for my friend. Only I was aware of her feelings for Panther. He was oblivious, almost mocking her unintentionally every time he brought another slut back to his room, his nightly sessions loud and energetic. It didn't help that Bullet's room was next to his. Many nights she'd climbed into my bed with me, her frantic sobs over Panther's latest fuck breaking my heart.

"We need to concentrate," Bullet said stiffly.

"You, concentrate?" Panther laughed. "I didn't think you were capable! They don't call blondes airheads for nothing."

"Oh, shut the fuck up you self-righteous, poncy twat!" Bullet hissed. I cringed and sighed.

"What the fuck climbed up your arse?"

"Well, it wasn't you unfortunately!" I snapped then stopped dead when I realised what I had said. I squeezed my eyes closed, cursing my inability to filter what came out.

Silence descended. Utter silence. Shit!

"What did you say?" Panther asked eventually.

"Uhh…."

"Shadow?" Panther asked again. I gritted my teeth and prayed.

"You know what?" I hissed into the mic as I ran up to the patio doors. "I need two Phantoms that can fucking get on. Panther, when are you going see past the end of your fucking nose?" I slid the device into the lock and waited for the green light to flash before clicking open the door. "And Bullet, firm tits and seduction are female traits we were given to use, so fucking use them for once!"

Her gasp met with Panther's silence. I rolled my eyes and quietly closed the door behind me. "Right I'm in." I eyed the room, registering the furniture layout. "And if I make it out of here alive, I want you both rocking the back of that van so hard that the earth moves for me too." I moved through the room towards the other door. "Got that?"

A grin twisted my mouth when Panther replied. "Yes, Ma'am. It would be a pleasure." When Bullet didn't answer, I smirked, imagining her passed out with her sniper rifle in her hands.

"Good boy. Now where are you?"

"Front of house. All clear."

"You've cleared already?"

"Yep. It's all yours. I'm off to find Bullet."

I chuckled at his eagerness. "Have fun."

"Oh, I intend to. I've been waiting to fuck the bitch for years."

I laughed harder when Bullet's gasp echoed in my ear.

I loved my friends. They made me happy. And when their giggles resonated in my ear ten minutes later, I unclipped my earpiece and walked into hell... and my past.

"Hello, Connie," he said softly.

My heart felt like it was going to rip from my chest and slap on the floor at my feet. I couldn't seem to comprehend anything, my mind chaotic and my brain numb, the clash making me faint and breathless. My head shook from side to side, my eyes blinking rapidly as though he was just an apparition that would vanish when my brain caught up with my eyes.

My hand came to my mouth, my palm pressing against my lips in an attempt to stop the vomit from exploding everywhere.

I was so shocked that I allowed my hands to be locked behind me in cuffs, my body hauled across the room and tossed into a chair as my stare refused me to recognise anything else happening around me.

Franco tied my ankles to the chair as my eyes tied me to the past.

"How could I have missed this?" My voice was quiet but I knew he heard me.

He shrugged as he walked towards me. I looked up at him as he bent towards me and tenderly placed a kiss on my cheek. "You are so beautiful," he whispered as his hand stroked over my hair. "You've done me and your mother proud."

It didn't make sense. None of it made sense. How was he alive? Here? Alive? I blinked numerous times, expecting him to fade out as reality sunk in, but the more my eyes focussed, the clearer he became.

As my brain caught up with my vision, I closed my eyes, everything becoming clear. "You!" I looked up at him with sadness. "You set it up. You arranged Mae's kidnapping. Not Franco." He stared at me, allowing me to finally see. "You finally got what you wanted."

He pulled in a breath and dragged out a chair from the table, placing it in front of me. "You always were the stupid one." He shook his head with mock laughter. "I knew when you found out and the Phantoms took you that you would one day be strong enough to take me on. Fair play to you, my dear, your plan nearly worked." He leaned forwards, placing his elbows on his knees. "Well, it would have done if your mother wasn't having an affair."

I gulped back the bile. "She wasn't supposed to have taken your car that night. Why, why did she?"

I wanted answers to what had gone wrong that night, and finally before I died, I was going to get them.

CHAPTER
TWENTY-SEVEN

'Face the Truth, Force the honesty.'

Daniel

SHE SHOULD HAVE been out by now. Something was wrong. Panther was blasting his mic, shouting her, calling her. Bullet was pacing, the air around her shimmering with the heated anger she spewed out.

"Shit," I heard Panther hiss out.

Bullet and I jumped into the van. My world rocked beneath me, my heart stuttering when I stared at the screen. A woman's silhouette sat in a chair. Two men were in the room with her. Another woman I presumed to be Helen was sitting in the lounge with Annie, playing on the floor.

Panther hit a red button on the console with the palm of his hand then grabbed Bullet's wrist when she picked up her sniper rifle. "That's not gonna work, you can't get a clear aim from here. We need to go in."

I stared wide-eyed when he passed her two shotguns. Walking over to me, he shoved two guns with suppressors attached into my hands. "You ever shot someone, Daniel?"

"Yep." I nodded, checking the ammo slot and getting a feel for each piece.

"Bullet!" Panther shouted as Bullet jumped out of the van and took off at speed towards the house. He caught up with her, tackling her to the ground. "Drag it in!" he growled as she grappled with him. "You know better than this. Calm down or you'll get her killed." She stared up at him, both fury and despair on her face. He tipped his head and cupped her cheek, his eyes slowly tracing every contour on her face. "I won't survive your death, never mind Shadow's." Her eyes widened on him, her lips parting as she sucked in a breath. "I've loved you for years, Elle, since the moment Frederik brought you back. Every single woman I have ever fucked was you, every face beneath me was yours. I hated you because I thought you were in love with Shadow. I thought you were fucking gay! I wanted you so damn much, with every single breath I took. You taunted me, made my cock so hard I was constantly in pain. But not just there, here," he snarled as he grabbed her hand and slapped it against his chest. "And now, now I finally understand and get what I have waited so fucking long for, you're hell bent on killing yourself. Don't make me lose my shit right now."

She choked out a sob, her chest heaving against his. She nodded.

I closed my eyes as his words curled inside me and tore me open.

"And now, now I finally understand and get what I have waited so fucking long for, you're hell bent on killing yourself."

My heart ached. Mae's smile, Mae's laughter, Mae's striking gaze, Mae's beautiful face, Mae's exquisite body, all of them assaulted me at once, crippling me, burning me up in their memory.

"I love you, lamb," I whispered to the stars. "I'll never stop loving you, ever. But I hope you can understand what I'm about to do, and why I need to do this."

Inhaling the last of the night air, I turned and walked away from the couple kissing on the ground and ran towards my childhood home, not seeing the tiny blue butterfly that landed on a stone next to where I was stood.

CHAPTER TWENTY-EIGHT

'Death is so final.'

Connie

I NARROWED MY eyes on him when he slipped a cigarette into his mouth and flicked open the lighter, the flame catching my attention. He cocked his head and lifted a brow. "You still smoke?"

"No, but right now I'll take one."

He nodded then turned to Franco. "Let the cuffs go."

Franco lifted a brow, "Is that wise?"

My father didn't hesitate. Spinning around he fixed Franco with a glare. "Do it!"

He shrugged and sighed then released my wrists. I rubbed at the sore skin then took the smoke from between his fingers and pulled in a drag, blowing it slowly into Franco's face. I smiled at him when his fist knocked my face sideways. "You always were a twat."

My dad laughed as Franco grabbed my jaw and snapped my face to his, his close proximity making me recoil. "And you always were a slut."

I nodded in agreement, pursing my lips. "Yes, I was. I still am. Is that why you wanted Mae and not me, 'cos she was innocent?"

He winked at me. "And she was so fucking delightful to break."

I lunged for him but the ties around my ankles saw me falling to the ground, my forehead bouncing off the floor tiles as lights blinked in my head. Franco laughed. "As Graham said, stupid."

"Fuck you!"

He smiled coldly, his eyes roaming down my body slowly. "If you insist."

"Don't even go there," my father spat out when Franco hoisted me up by my hair.

Rolling his eyes and huffing, Franco pulled the chair back up and threw me back onto it. "I can wait." He chuckled, leaning against the worktop and folding his arms over his chest.

"Me too." I smirked at him. "I'll finally get to shoot off that tiny dick of yours." And I didn't mean give him a wank.

He nodded, his smug smile making my blood heat. "And I'm gonna make sure to shoot it all over your pretty little face."

"Get out!" my dad bellowed at him. Franco snapped his head around, frowning at him. "Get out before I fucking destroy *your* pretty little face!"

I narrowed my eyes, watching the play, wondering how long my father had dominated their relationship. "Were all the decisions yours?" I asked him as Franco shook his head and left.

He sighed then turned back to me. "Most of them."

"Why? Why Mae?"

He regarded me for a while before taking another cigarette, lighting it then handing it to me. He lit his own, blowing a few smoke rings into the air before he leant back in his chair, crossed his legs and dropped his eyes to his lap.

"I admit to you, I was a crap husband." I nodded when he lifted his eyes to mine. "But I was always a loving father, Con.

Always."

"Were."

He nodded slowly. "Yes." He shrugged, taking another drag. "It all became quite a mess really. I was called in one day, at work. It must have been sixteen, seventeen years ago now. I was to go undercover to gain evidence in a sex slave business that had come under the radar of the Met."

"Daniel's father."

"Yes, and Franco. The force supplied me with references from criminals who were already locked up, reducing their sentences and giving me an in with Franco and the Shepherds."

"Shepherds? Plural?"

He squinted at me. "Yes, Robert and Miriam. Daniel's parents."

"His parents? As in father *and* mother?"

He pursed his lips. "He never told you about his mother?"

"No," I whispered. Things started to slot into place. Miriam's death, Daniel's refusal to talk of his mother but then his next words exploded into me and everything snapped together.

"I was having an affair with Miriam. I loved her."

"What?" I choked out as I stared at him with wide eyes. I groaned and rubbed my face with my hands. "I never saw it. I... *Fuck!*"

"Miriam hated it all. She hated that Robert had got Daniel involved. She threatened to go to the police with everything. She was a ticking time bomb with the stuff she knew. She would have ruined it all, years of hard work, the money we had made, the clients we had gathered; everything including our freedom would have been lost. Robert wanted to get rid of her, his own wife."

"Talk about a cliché," I spat at him.

He nodded but didn't offer words to my hatred. His eyes saddened as he looked to the floor. "Daniel overheard Miriam and myself in her room one night. He didn't know it was me. He went to find his father at a casino he ran at the time and told him about his mother's lover. Robert knew it was me but he never told Daniel. He turned it all around to look like Miriam was trying to kill Helen and Daniel, trying to get rid of her kids so she could run off with her lover and ruin the family business. He told him Miriam was just out for herself, that she wanted nothing but the man she was in love with and that she was going to go to the police and tell them everything to get both Robert and Daniel out of her way. Daniel thought I was having an affair with Franco's wife. Fuck, even Franco thought I was."

I leaned forwards, trying to hold on to my hatred. "You allowed Franco to keep thinking that to save Miriam."

"Yes." He nodded but swallowed when he realised I finally understood.

"And in that allowance, you sacrificed your children. You chose a woman over your fucking daughters!"

"Yes." He stared at me, no regret or no guilt covering him.

I shook my head, my mouth open in disgust or shock, or maybe even rage, it was all clashing together and I was unable to process anything.

"The night the Phantoms came for me. I thought it was over your debts to Franco, but it wasn't, was it?"

He shook his head slowly. "No. It was Robert who had sent them to take you from me, like I had taken his wife from him. I didn't realise what they were doing at first. I heard Robert had taken out a contract on you both and I tried to protect you as much as I could but they never came."

"THEY DID COME!" I screamed at him. "They came and they exchanged mine and Mae's life for the promise that I would go with them at fifteen."

He nodded. "I know this now. But you must understand, it's rare for a Phantom to ever do what they did that day. If they came, you were dead!" He shook his head, tears pooling in his eyes. "They never ever took a child and trained her up for two years then sent her back."

"They took *me*." I spat at him. "Isaac took me, and trained me. It was only his love for me that gave Mae a chance." A tear trickled down my cheek and I swiped at it angrily. "I knew what was to come when I hit fifteen. I knew there was no point hiding, or even denying them. But Isaac, he came, time after time, training me in readiness for them. He would sneak out, sneak to see me. For eighteen months he showed me how to fight, how to plot, how to shoot and finally how to let someone into my heart after hating for so long. And I did it, every - fucking - damn - day, so Mae could live a full life! Isaac risked his life for me, and he continues to do so every day. That… *That* is love! Not some piss take that ruins people… and families!""

He continued to watch me, his face pale, and his eyes so very sad. "Then I hit fifteen and they came for me. It was six months before you died that they told me all about your sordid fucking life, and your willingness to give up your children for a woman you were fucking!"

"And you plotted my death?"

"You're damn right I did!" I spat at him. "But you… you even ruined that! Do you know how many nights I have slept properly since my mistakes killed my own mother, and which then lead to the life Mae was to lead? Do you? *DO YOU?*" He blinked at me. "None. Not one single night."

"Your mother was having an affair." He looked away, pain in his eyes. I wanted to laugh at his double standards. "The night I was due to be at work, she came running into the kitchen with some half-baked story about needing to get to hospital because a friend of hers had been taken ill. There was something wrong with her car and she begged to take mine."

I squeezed my eyes closed, the pain inside ripping me apart. "Don't," I whispered.

"I didn't know, Connie. I DIDN'T KNOW! She picked him up and they were on their way to some smutty hotel to fuck!"

"No," I choked out, each word slicing into me deeper and deeper until I could feel my soul bleeding.

"I knew then, after she died with her lover, after Miriam was killed at the hands of her only son, after your lives were put at risk, after my death was on the cards, even after the dreadful things I had done, that it was time to go. I took the opportunity when the bodies in the car were too badly burnt to be recognised and it was presumed that I was with her. I walked away. From everything. From death."

"From me, from *Mae*! You chose your own selfish needs instead of us!" My mouth watered and I breathed against the violent need to vomit. "And let me guess." I licked at my lips, holding him with my eyes. "Franco found out. Robert found you." His nod gave me the encouragement to voice the sickening knowledge that battered into me. "And you gave Mae to Robert in exchange for your life."

He stared at me, his throat bobbing before he nodded. I wanted to die right then. I wanted it all to end, for life to be over, for the pain of it all to cease. So when he lifted the gun, I didn't move. I only smiled.

Yet when my father's blood sprayed across my face, the bullet forced by his own hand firing through his brain and then the gun slipping from his fingers and onto the floor, I prayed that him taking his own life would see him in hell because I wanted him nowhere near my sister.

CHAPTER
TWENTY-NINE

'Time to say goodbye.'

Daniel

FRANCO SMIRKED AT me, his arms pinned behind his back as Panther held him. My eyes shifted around my childhood home, the entrance hall exactly as I remembered it. Family portraits still hung from the walls in chronological order up the stairs, the awful chandelier my mother had insisted on still swung from the chain and the air still smelt of sin and corruption. Voices echoed around me, women's screams, men's moans, girls' whimpers, my own cries and Helen's frantic sobbing when she found me with our mother's lifeless body.

"Where is she?" Panther snarled at Franco, his grip on his face making Franco appear deformed.

He snorted and shook his head. "It doesn't matter. You're too late. She's gone."

"No." I grabbed him by the throat, my fingers so tight they threatened to puncture his neck any second. "She was here. Where is she? Where's Helen?"

He just smiled at me, his smug expression snapping my patience. He started to choke as I leant into him and squeezed tighter. "If you've hurt her, I will personally rip your heart out and force feed it you."

His lips were turning blue, the colour so satisfying to my dark side. The power to hold someone's life in your hands, to decide whether they lived or died was the ultimate pleasure. Watching as the heart took its final beat, the soul shrivelling in their eyes and each organ shutting down one by one was euphoric and rapturous.

"Daniel," Panther warned. "We need him, let him…"

We all froze when a gunshot rang out from the direction of the kitchen. Panther's eyes shot to mine as Bullet took off at speed.

Franco laughed as I released him, his gasps for breath squeaking with his amusement. "He did it then."

The kitchen door opened and Connie stepped out. She was covered in blood, her face pale and startling against the deep crimson.

"Shadow?" Bullet asked as she held Connie's upper arms, her voice tight as her eyes rapidly scanned her friend.

"I'm okay," Connie whispered. "I'm okay."

Her gaze turned to Franco before she slowly walked over to him. "Tell me why he killed himself."

Franco looked saddened for a moment before it disappeared and he tilted his head, mocking her, a cruel smirk twisting his face. "Well if you think he did it because of guilt, think again. He was dying… painfully."

He and Panther flew backwards when Connie smashed her fist into his face. "He had cancer didn't he?"

Franco nodded as Panther shifted them both upright. "Brain cancer. He was going the same way as his daughter. Ironic huh?"

"You bastard!" she spat. "He didn't deserve to die so fucking easily. He deserved nothing but pain. He was a coward!"

"Shadow," Bullet urged as she took Connie's hand. Connie shook her off and stepped into Franco.

"Tell me where Annie is."

He shook his head slowly. "You'll never find her."

Connie took a deep breath and looked at Panther. "The interrogation room ready?"

"Yep."

"Take him. I'll be over in an hour."

Panther nodded and pulled Franco towards the door before turning back round. "Isaac's on his way. I'll take the van, he'll drive you."

"Yeah. I..." She closed her eyes and shivered, her skin becoming paler by the second. "I need a few moments."

He nodded and left. Bullet pulled Connie into her arms, hugging her. "Are you sure? I can stay."

"No, go. I'm fine."

Bullet sighed, debating whether to follow orders or deny Connie. "I'll stay with her," I offered.

"I need a few moments alone." I nodded when she gestured towards the kitchen with her chin. "Time to say goodbye."

"Are you okay?"

She sighed and nodded slowly. "Yeah." She looked like she wanted to say something, the anguish written on her face but she smiled softly and disappeared into the kitchen, closing the door quietly behind her.

Ascending the stairs, I smiled at each picture, each photograph of my family making my heart heavier and heavier the more I climbed. Then I reached their bedroom. My mouth dried as I slid the handle and pushed open the door.

It was the same, exactly as we had left it fifteen years ago, the day after my mother died. The day of my eighteenth birthday. The day I killed her.

My feet seemed to be glued to the spot, forbidding me to go any further. The bed was still made, her perfumes and cosmetics were still laid out on the dresser waiting for her to spray liberally as she always had. Her gown still hung from the bathroom door, the tiny blue butterfly silk choking me.

Finally taking a step inside, I walked over to the mural that hung over her bed. Each butterfly appeared to move as the rising sun sprung from the ground and blasted the room in light and heat. Reaching towards it, I stroked the tip of my finger over the largest.

"Holly Blue," her voice whispered to me as I watched her gently pin the dead insect to her project. "They usually live in groups, Dan. But this one, she was on her own, lonely. She called to me, asked me to take her to the others."

I nodded, not really interested. I thought it was cruel how she would kill them then stick them to a piece of wood, as though relishing in the ability to kill a living creature.

"Can I go see Thomas now? He's waiting for me." She scowled at me. I lowered my eyes, contrite. "I'm sorry, Mummy."

"Look how pretty it looks in death, Daniel. How very peaceful she is now." I nodded again, looking up at the poor thing. "It's something quite spectacular to watch the life drain from a living thing, a thing so full of beauty. Watch as you take its beauty away. Its soul."

My stomach turned. I hated her when she was like this, she frightened me. Not because of how she would take a creature's life, but how the day always ended when she was on a high.

She cupped my cheek and I stilled, my body automatically clenching with her soft touch. "You, Daniel, you are beautiful. I often wonder how you will look when your life drains away, how it would make me feel to watch your soul wither in your eyes."

Her hand glided over my throat, her fingers curling around my neck so she could feel the throb of my pulse, something she always liked to do, something that always excited her, she always said. A sob stuck in my throat when I felt the warm trickle between my legs, the material of my trousers sticking to my privates as my urine soaked me.

Mother tutted, shaking her head in disappointment. "Oh dear, look what you have done."

I took a step back and grabbed her hand when she fiddled with my belt. "No, Mummy, I'll do it."

I cried out when her hand slapped my face. "You never deny me, Daniel. I warrant your respect. Are you an ungrateful wretch?"

"No, Mummy," I replied automatically, dropping my hands to my side as tears trickled from my eyes.

"You owe me your life, Daniel. Always remember who gave you life, and who can take it away so easily."

"I'm sorry."

"And who can take Helen from you," she whispered.

I squeezed my eyes closed as she pulled down my trousers and pants, my throat closing in as her hands then drifted upwards….

I jolted forward, vomit curling up my throat as I made a dash for the bathroom, my stomach contents hurtling into the toilet.

Splashing my face with water I stormed from the room, refusing to look anymore.

Connie was taking her time. I thought she would have been finished with her father by now. We needed to hurry and find Annie and Helen.

I took one last look at my family as I descended the stairs, knowing it was time to say goodbye. It was finally time to let her go. She couldn't hurt me any longer. She had degraded me, damaged me, and made me cry time after time when my childhood should have been something to look back on and smile at, but as she had once told me, it had been beautiful to watch the life drain from her eyes, her soul snuffed out so easily. And her death had been the start of many for me. She made me and she ended me.

Pushing the kitchen door open slowly so as not to disturb Connie in the final moments with her father, I walked in quietly.

Time seemed to stop as my heart beat sped up. Blood roared through my veins, its pounding in my ears deafening as the scene before me registered in my brain.

"Hello, Daniel," my father said. His eyes were cold, so cold.

His lip was curled in disgust, his chest heaving with hatred as he pushed the blade into Connie's shoulder. She hissed at the pain when he screwed it further and further into her flesh. Her legs buckled but he yanked her back up, pushing the knife deeper into her with the movement.

"Father. Stop."

He laughed. "It's time to end the game, son." I flinched when he threw a dice at me. It hit me and dropped to the floor, bouncing along the floor tiles and coming to rest against one of the kitchen cupboards. "Roll."

I stared at him. "What?"

"Roll," he repeated. "Odds, she dies. Evens..." He smirked, his eyes lighting with cruelty. "You die."

CHAPTER THIRTY

'In the end, we only have the beginning.'

Connie

"ROLL!" HE BARKED again, making me jump, making the knife sink deeper. "You like to play games, Daniel. So let's play."

I couldn't see a way out of his hold without tearing a hole right through me.

"I'm not playing your stupid fucking games," Daniel answered. "Let her go and we'll talk."

"Talk?" Robert laughed. I moaned as the knife jerked and closed my eyes as everything around me swayed. "What is there to talk about? You? Me? Our relationship? Oh come on, we've never really had one, Daniel."

"What?" Daniel shook his head from side to side. "I did your bidding. I took your orders. I killed for you."

"No, Daniel. You killed because you enjoyed the hunt, the death of those you held in your hands. Don't seek redemption for being guilty, seek the truth of who you are."

"The truth? You have no idea of the truth. You never did. You were a fool, a coward who never looked at what you saw."

"No. Not this again. I never believed your lies because that's exactly what they were, lies."

I clenched my teeth when Daniel took a step towards us and Robert rammed a gun into my temple. "Keep going, son. I'd love to see if her blood is red or black."

Daniel flicked his eyes to mine. His jaw was clenched so hard I worried for his teeth. He stepped back and lifted his hands. "Fine." He took a deep breath and snatched up the dice. "And just for the record... *Father*. Our mother wasn't only a child abuser, she was an adulterer, a liar and the biggest manipulator out there. She fooled you, she fooled Franco." He turned to me, his painful expression finding mine before returning to Robert. "She fooled Graham. But she was definitely no fool herself. She played you all. The queen of games. And not one of you could see her jumping from one bed to the other... including mine."

He turned and threw the dice. It skittered along the worktop, rebounding off the cupboard and came to rest beside him, spinning wildly before it dropped on one side. His eyes lowered before rising slowly. He glanced at me, his eyes flicking with an ache I had never seen before. My heart threatened to give me a coronary. My breathing became stunted and I swallowed back the taste of death.

He gave me a soft smile. "I loved her, swan. She was my salvation. Please be sure to tell her that when you join her."

I gasped, the blood draining from me. Not here, not like this. I wanted to tell Isaac so many things before I died. I wanted to hold him, and make him feel me, make him understand that my heart was his, all his. But as I looked at Daniel, our eyes meeting for the last time, I nodded. "Why the swan?" Strangely it was the only thing I wanted to know in the moments before my death.

His smile grew wider. "Because you're the most stunning assassin of all living creatures. So beautiful, yet so dangerous beneath it all. You don't deserve this life, just like Mae didn't."

He sighed, holding my eyes for a fraction longer before he slowly lifted his eyes to Robert. "Even," he whispered.

What? No! My heart stopped when Robert removed the gun from my head and pointed it at Daniel. "Goodbye, son. Well played."

Daniel stood still as two bullets hit his chest. His eyes widened as his mouth dropped open. Blood seeped from him, marring his clean white shirt, spreading over him so fast my brain couldn't decipher what it was. His gaze moved to me as his legs stuttered and he dropped to his knees. "Tell her, Connie. Tell her."

I nodded, my head shaking as a sob forced free from deep within me. "I promise."

He smiled, falling to his side on the ground. "Let her go, Connie. It's time to open your heart. To forgive yourself. Set her free, set yourself free… and let go."

Robert dropped to the floor beside me, a bullet hole appearing in his forehead, weeping blood down over his face as Isaac appeared in the doorway, his gun trained on Robert, his eyes very much holding me.

I couldn't move. I didn't know whether to stare at Isaac, his beauty and his love the only thing my eyes wanted, or Daniel, the one my heart was telling me to go to.

My feet finally moved, taking me to Daniel. I dropped to the floor next to him and pulled him to me. "Daniel? Daniel? Hold on."

He opened his eyes and I gasped at the complete peace behind them. He was staring beyond me, a tender smile lifting his lips, his eyes so full of love. "No," he choked out. "She's here. Take care of Annie. I never deserved her. She deserves you. Love her, swan. Love her so hard." I nodded, drowning in my own tears, the salt stinging my lips, my choked sobs loud in the silence of the room. He lifted his hand, stroking his knuckles over my cheek as his eyes closed. "I was her decimation. She is my salvation."

His hand fell to my lap, his fingers uncurling to reveal a small blue butterfly as a smile touched his lips and his soul joined its mate.

"Tell her I miss her," I whispered as I leant down and placed my lips on his head. I curled his fingers back around the butterfly, holding his hand closed around it. "Tell her you love her, Daniel. And listen when she tells you. Because you do deserve her. You do deserve her love."

Isaac lifted me and pulled me to him tightly, growling when he saw the knife still stuck in my shoulder. "Shit, my love." I rested my head on his shoulder as he led me out of the room. "I was rather fond of that t-shirt."

I smiled and looked down to the counter. Stopping Isaac, I stared at the dice. "Oh, Christ." Stretching my hand out, I ran a finger over the three white dots, the odd number that had issued my death warrant.

Life truly was a cruel game. Death granted at the roll of a dice. But love; well that was what won the game... and sacrifice? That granted salvation.

CHAPTER THIRTY-ONE

'And finally, in salvation we find redemption.'

Connie

I WATCHED ISAAC work on Franco, not really registering anything that was happening, not hearing Franco's torturous screams, or even seeing the pools of blood gathered below where he hung from the chain. Isaac was hard, the brutal suffering he inflicted arousing him. He loved pain, he always had, and in one way, I understood why he had made sure I enjoyed it too. He'd moulded me into his ultimate plaything, a toy that could handle his wild side, and a wife that could give his heart and soul nourishment.

Daniel's death hit me hard. I couldn't stop the deep sorrow inside me. What the hell was this world, this life? The only thought granting me peace was that Mae finally had what she had always looked for. Daniel was now with her. I had to believe that, not just for my sanity, but for Annie's future.

What was I going to tell her? I had broken the promise I'd given her when I had told her I would bring back her daddy. She'd lost both parents, her young innocence taken away so early. But then again, so had I, and I had survived, yet that thought didn't help, it made my heart sink deeper.

I knew I had told Daniel I would be the one granting him death, but I also knew that I could never do that to Annie. Yet, fate had decided that my choice wasn't acceptable and had secured what was to be taken from the beginning. But where did the end take me now? Would there ever be an end?

I felt that roll of the dice as distinctly as Daniel. The odd number three should have been my end, but Daniel had chosen it to be my beginning.

"I want the white picket fence, Isaac."

He turned to me, my sudden odd words creasing his brow. His head tilted to one side, his eyes regarding me, scrutinising me. Blood dripped from his fingers, the scalpel he held twisting between his fingers as he twirled it round. His bare torso was lined in blood, his contoured abs supplying valleys for the red fluid to ride along.

"I want a puppy," I continued as I gazed at him, sadness overwhelming me. "I want to celebrate Christmas with Annie. I want to be able to answer a knock at the front door without having to shove a knife into the back of my jeans first."

He continued to watch me, listening to every word as his expression softened and his breathing regulated.

"I want to take Annie around the world, show her things that only the most privileged witness. I want to play fight in the summer, with hose pipes and buckets. I want to sledge in the snow, laugh under the stars. I want to roll down grassy hills and hear Annie's laugh every day. But more than that."

He watched me walk towards him, my slow steps echoing loudly in the silent concrete room. "I want to be married, like a *normal* husband and wife. I want to wear your ring. I want to be... I want to be *just* a woman. I'm so tired, so tired of this fight.

Tired of hurting, both others and myself. I'm tired of struggling to breathe under the suffocation of our lives."

He cupped my face when I reached him. I didn't care that he smeared me with blood. I didn't care that Franco was witnessing what was happening between husband and wife. "I want to be happy, Isaac."

He stared at me, his pure green eyes worshipping me. The hand holding my face slid upwards and sank into my hair, before he twisted it and pulled my face to his. He didn't speak, he just crashed his mouth over mine. His soft lips were brutal, hard and punishing. His growl into my mouth was loud and demanding as he pulled me harder into him.

I pulled away and blinked at him. "Say something."

"I want to watch the sun set with my wife, whilst Annie chases the puppy. I want to watch your face as you laugh. I want to see the light in your eyes when I finally make you mine and only mine. I want to give you all of me, Con. I want all of you. No more sharing, no more jobs, no more Phantoms. I want to close the white picket gate at night, and lay beside you until the sun comes up. I want it all, my love. But most of all, I just want you. I will follow you into hell, but until then, I will follow any direction your life goes because I'm right beside you, whatever you want."

I couldn't help but smile at him. "You mean that. You'd give it all up?"

He stared at me, his eyebrows lifting in astonishment. "Of course I would. I know you're ready, Connie. You've been ready for a long time. But it was only ever you who could put Shadow in the shadows. Your heart is the only thing that can reinvent the Phantom inside you. All I've ever wanted is for you to be happy, I thought you knew that, understood me."

"I do," I whispered. "But the Phantoms are your life."

"You. You, my love, are my life. You and now Annie. I won't even blink at making you happy. All I ever want is to witness that beautiful fucking smile of yours every morning and every evening. That's all. That's it. That's me." He kissed the tip of my nose. "I'm quite simple really."

I chuckled and nodded. "You are the simplicity in complexity, darling."

He shrugged and nodded. "That too. Now if you'll excuse me, I have work to do." He winked and blew me a kiss before I turned and ventured back over to the chair in the corner of the room.

"Now, Franco. I'm bored." Isaac sighed. "Let's liven this up."

She actually opened the front door to us when Isaac and I pulled up the thin gravel driveway. Isaac quirked an eyebrow at me before pulling the car up to a stop in front of the door.

"Well, she looks full of the joys of spring," he mocked when Helen stared at us with a bored expression.

"Mmm," I agreed, sighing heavily.

"She looks delightful." His lip curled when his gaze roved down over her body then back up to her stern face. "How would you like to do this, my love, quick or slow?"

Stifling a yawn, I rolled my head round my shoulders. "Fast and easy. I just want a hot bubble bath, a foot rub and your tongue in my pussy."

Isaac snatched up his gun and grabbed the door handle. I laughed, holding his arm and pushing the gun back on to his lap. "Whoa, Stud. Slow down, we have to think of Annie."

"Well hurry. I need you. I've been on rations."

I gawped at him, my mouth wide with shock. "What?"

He shrugged, almost embarrassed as his eyes lowered to his lap. "They're not you, Connie. They never have been. And to be honest, they bore me. My wife, well, she excites me. She makes me laugh in the bedroom, she even breaks wind when I tickle her." He nodded slowly as though proud of my ability to fart. "She makes my cock feel absolutely fucking fantastic but more than that, she loves me, she adores me. And I've realised after all this time, that's what makes it what it is with you. Your love, and my love for you. And there is no greater climax than coming deep inside of you as your eyes give me all your thoughts, your soul and your heart. That's what makes me yours, and that's what makes us fucking awesome in bed."

He ran his fingertip across my cheekbone, collecting the tears that fell. "Are you ready?"

"I need to do this on my own."

He smiled, nodding. "I'll come in and get the munchkin, then she's all yours."

"Are you sure you want to do this?" I asked as I looked in his eyes. He shook his head in confusion. "Annie. Bringing Annie into our family."

"My love, Annie is already in our family. She has been ever since she was born. She's part of you, and that makes her part of us. I want her to have that puppy, and days on the beach, and water fights. I want to make her laugh, I want to tickle her until she can't breathe. And I want to watch her pick up her first ever baby and sing to her. I want to be the one who walks her down the aisle when she falls in love, I want to shoot at the prick that breaks her heart and I want her to grant me a grandbaby. Because she's part of *you*, Connie."

"You know," I whispered, unable to lift my voice higher with the emotion coursing through me. "An hour ago, I was regretting what life had given me. But I'd do it all again, three thousand times over, because it gave me you. I look at Mae's life, and yes, although it was my choices that gave her hers, she had to wait until death to find what I've had since I was thirteen. And that in itself, gives me cause to be grateful. I have never known a man love a woman as much as you love me. You went against the rules and took the most severe punishment for me. You killed your father for me. But above all that, you love me. Me, the ordinary girl who had to make a choice on a dark winter's night. A choice that would change everything. But take me back there right now and I will pick that same choice."

"Will you stop," he whined. "I'm seriously thinking about making love to you now." His brows furrowed. "You know, like… slowly and softly." He stared at me in shock with himself.

"We could try," I whispered.

His pursed his lips in thought. "You mean, no spanking, no belt, no yanking your hair? Just…."

"Just us."

He leaned into me, his warm breath whispering over me as he slid his fingers around the side of my neck. "I'd love to."

I beamed at him before flicking my eyes to an even more bored Helen. Her arms were crossed across her chest whilst she waited for us. I blew out a breath and opened the door.

"Let's do this. Let's go fetch our little person and finish it."

"I'm right behind you, my love. For the very last time, Shadow." He nodded seriously, giving me the courage I needed to do this.

Closing my eyes briefly, I pulled in a fortifying breath. "Time to reach the end square."

EPILOGUE

'Life goes on. Our hearts continue to grow. And our souls will forever link us to those departed.'

Eighteen years later

Connie

I GRIT MY teeth, pacing back and forth. I was going to kill him. Where the hell was he?

Bullet rolled her eyes at me. "Where is he? Annie's up soon."

Checking my watch again like that would stop time and put things on hold until Isaac arrived, I saw it was five minutes since I'd looked five minutes ago.

I raised my hands in the air and took a breath when I saw Isaac racing across the university car park towards us. "Where have you been?" I grumbled as I automatically went to fix his tie.

"Sorry," he panted, trying to catch his breath. "Annie couldn't find her speech."

I narrowed my eyes. "Annie's been here for over an hour."

"Yes," he said slowly, removing my hands from his tie and redoing it. "And she sent me back for her speech."

"Fine." I pulled him up the stairs and into the main building. "But hurry, she's on any minute."

He held out a piece of paper, obviously Annie's speech. "Well she needs this."

I smiled at the sweat dripping from him, his hands shaking, his pale face tight, his flapping hands and his teeth gnawing on his bottom lip. Annie had been the making of Isaac. They doted on each other. Ever since we took her home that night eighteen years ago, she had him wrapped around her little finger. They were inseparable.

"Isaac, darling." I reached out and took his hand in mine. "She will be fine. I promise."

He nodded stiffly, swallowing heavily. "I know. I'm more nervous than she is," he laughed.

We took the seats reserved for us near the front. The principal was rambling about this year's graduates, how well they had developed over the four years they had attended university.

My eyes wandered, landing on Annie by the side of the stage area. My brow quirked at the man with her. He was tall, dark-haired and gorgeous. Annie had grown into a stunning twenty two year old woman. She had mine and Mae's eyes, our black hair and Mae's curves. She had Daniel's full lips and height, but her temperament was very much her father's, as was her strength and courage. Her heart was all Mae but her head, her intelligence, was Daniel's. She was the epitome of them. They had each given her the very best parts of them, and they lived in her.

The guy had his hand on Annie's arm, talking to her. She was shaking her head, her face stern as she refused to look at him. It was obvious they were arguing.

"Please tell me you brought at least one gun, my love," Isaac whispered in my ear as he watched the same scene unfolding.

I nudged him with my elbow, trying to stifle my laughter

when Annie was introduced onto the stage. She snatched her arm from the dickhead and strolled up to the podium, her elegant grace holding the attention of every man in the audience.

She smiled out to everyone. Isaac lifted the paper and flapped it at her. She reached out then shook her head and smiled at him before addressing the audience again.

"Hello, I'm Annie Shepherd," she started. "I did have a speech all readily prepared. But you know what, it was a load of shite." The audience laughed as Annie shrugged. "Life doesn't come prepared with instructions or written on a piece of paper. We make it up as we go along. We take each hurdle and we jump it and carry on to the next one. If we don't manage to get over that one, we take a few steps back and attempt it again. But we never give up. We can't give up."

She looked to me and Isaac and smiled. "I lost both parents as a very small child. I'm not the only one; there are others out there who have lost loved ones. I don't look at losses, I look at what I gained because of their lives *and* their deaths."

She smiled at everyone, her beautiful bright blue eyes smiling with her. "I often wondered as a child, and still do, what made each of us who we are, why each person would choose different options in life. Why one person deems death as the end, and another thinks of it as the start of a different journey. How one considers it acceptable, sometimes even enjoyable, to take another's life, whilst another would actually give up their own life to let another live."

I looked around the auditorium, smiling as Annie stole everyone, their eyes regarding her, their ears listening to her, their attention with her and only her.

"As you can gather, yes, I chose to study psychology. And I'm very proud to say I graduated with honours. But I often wonder if life had taken me on a different route, what would I be doing now?"

Her tongue slid across her bottom lip and her eyes moved to Isaac, a secret smile curling the corners of her mouth. "Would I be a killer? What would life have done to me to make me want to feel the final beat of someone's heart in my hands?"

Isaac sighed satisfactorily beside me. "You know," he whispered as he leant into me. "Are you sure she isn't ours?"

I chuckled "I've never known anyone like her."

Isaac nodded.

"But as one side clashes with the other, is it in our genes what life decides for us, or is it our own choices through life that determines what we become? Does our upbringing have any impact on our adulthood? As we take on our parents features when we are born, do we also take their characteristics? If your father was a killer and your mother the most innocent and loving woman out there, what would that make you?"

"That would make you Annie Shepherd," Isaac scoffed.

"Would you be a compassionate killer?" Annie continued. "Would you only kill the most deserving?"

"Yes, you would Annie Shepherd." Isaac agreed.

I looked to my lap and smiled.

"Would you feel empathy for those you kill? Or do you relish in their deaths, taking into consideration what your victim has done to hurt others."

"Well, you always kiss them goodnight, Annie Shepherd," Isaac mumbled with a small chuckle.

"The organs of the body were genetically developed to work with one another, each connected by a matrix of cells carried respectively through our blood system. But what if, in some, each organ works against the other. What if your head told you one thing and your heart the other. Your head tells you to take this disturbed piece of shit that raped your sister or mother and blot out their existence, but your heart tells you that maybe this vile man has something genetic or psychological inside them that drowns all reasoning within them and they need someone to understand what makes them this way. What do you have then?"

"Annie Shepherd," Isaac and I said together.

"And that's what I will be studying and learning from as I

work with the police force to determine serial killers, criminals and kidnappers, and how they work."

"So you can fill that little black book, munchkin," Isaac snorted.

The audience erupted into a mass of applause, every person standing, Isaac and I included.

I grinned up at her proudly. She winked at me then descended the stairs.

"That's my girl," Isaac puffed out proudly.

Bullet snorted. "Well, with a mixture of her parents and you two, there's no wonder she turned out to be the deadliest assassin this planet has ever known."

Isaac grinned proudly. "Yes, she did."

I laughed, nudging him. "After me, darling."

"Oh," he nodded wildly. "Of course, my love. You know, I often wonder what she would have become if you hadn't taken a sledgehammer to that white picket fence you wanted and returned to the dark side."

"You think she'd have become a vet or something?"

Isaac and Bullet laughed loudly. "Annie? A vet?" Isaac barked out. "There's a reason her codename is Butterfly, and it's not for her closeness to nature." I chuckled, nodding my head in agreement. "It's her ability to blend into the background. Feed from the innocent. Her beauty attracts everyone, dragging them in and under until she wraps those delicate wings around them and snaps their necks."

"Hey." Annie smiled, kissing both Isaac and myself on the cheeks as she flung her arms around us.

"Brilliant speech, munchkin." Isaac beamed at her proudly. She smiled back at him and nodded. "You ready for dinner now?"

She pursed her lips. "Do you mind if I give it a miss. The Kitchen is having a barbeque and I promised to help out."

Isaac rolled his eyes. "Why do you help out at that homeless place? It's your graduation."

"Isaac," Annie grumbled at him. "These people need someone to care, otherwise what do they have in life? We weren't all granted opportunities in life. There would be so many homeless dying without places like The Kitchen."

"Fine!" Isaac relented, holding his hands up in surrender, knowing it was useless to argue. "What about tomorrow, then?"

Annie lifted a brow at him. "Uhh, tomorrow we're taking out that fucking knob that raped his neighbour's little girl, remember?"

"Oh yeah. Breakfast then?"

"Breakfast it is," Annie agreed with a smile.

A tall stunning blonde-haired girl came running up to Annie, slipping her arm around her and pulling her in close. "You busy later?"

"I'm free after my shift at The Kitchen."

Blondie nodded. "See you at mine after?"

"Sure," Annie replied. The blonde winked and wandered back into the crowd, shouting over her shoulder. "Oh, I've invited Simon as well, that okay?"

The smile on Annie's lips told me everything. "Of course, the more the merrier."

Isaac lifted a brow at me and wrapped his arm around my shoulder, pulling me close. "Maybe she does take after you after all."

"Nah," I replied. "She's all Mae's heart and Daniel's head. The shepherd and the lamb."

"And the exquisite blue butterfly."

THE END

Turn over for a sneak peak at

The Beginning of
Connie and Isaac

Book 3 in the Blue Butterfly Series

Coming Spring 2015

PROLOGUE

Isaac

February 2004. Aged 19.

PULLING MY COAT further around me, I turned up the heating dial, shivering against the ice that formed on the inside of the car window, never mind the outside. The music coming from the speakers was quiet and I wanted nothing more than to blast it higher to drown out my thoughts.

I tapped the steering wheel to the beat, shifting my glance to the upstairs window of the house I was watching. Light still glowed from behind the thin curtains, the shadow of a figure moving around.

I needed to wait until they were asleep, make this easier. For some reason, amongst others, this job felt different. I couldn't put my finger on it. Although the targets didn't sit well with me, it wasn't just that that was grieving me. Yet, here I sat, waiting to do what I did best.

The shadow in the window appeared to be dancing. I smiled, watching the figure move to what I presumed to be an upbeat tune. The way her hand rested to her mouth I knew she currently had hold of a hairbrush, singing for her life to whichever song her preferences had her listening to.

I grabbed my ringing phone from the passenger seat beside

me, rolling my eyes at the number displayed on the screen.

"Yep."

"Hey. You back tonight? The place is flooded with pussy, man. Your father's decided to hold a party for some unknown reason."

I couldn't hold back the growl. I knew the exact reason for his party. "No. I'm out."

"What?" Joel scoffed. "Pussy, Isaac, lots and lots of glorious pussy. What the hell's wrong with you?"

I rubbed at my face, suddenly tired. My eyes flicked back to the house and I sighed. "I dunno. It's this fucking job. Doesn't feel right."

Joel was silent for a moment. "It's just a job, man. In, kill, out. That's it, that's all it ever is."

"They're thirteen, Joel. I mean shit, they're kids."

"Since when did you develop a conscience?" he mumbled, but I knew he understood.

"Since I got sent to do the dirty jobs."

"You gonna nail 'em first?"

"What the fuck?" I spat, my lip curling in disgust. "Thirteen, Joel. Thir-teen!"

"Fresh pussy." I stared gobsmacked at the pattern the ice had formed on the window, tracing the developing web with my gaze as Joel jabbered on. "And hell, if I know girls nowadays, you might not even be their first."

"You sick fuck!" I shook my head, wondering what the hell I saw in Joel as a friend at times. "You're gonna regret saying that when I get back."

"Yeah, yeah," he mumbled. "Becca's here."

"Yeah? Go fuck her then, she'll more than oblige." I ended the call, throwing my phone back on the seat.

Glancing back at the house I murmured a groan when I saw the upper light extinguish. "Fuck!"

I climbed from the car, looking around to make sure I wasn't being watched, and walked around the back of the house, scaling the high gate and dropping to the ground on the other side, my feet skidding slightly on the frosty ground. My brow quirked at the large fountain standing proud in the centre of the garden, masses of bushes doing half my job for me and blocking me from neighbouring eyes.

My feet dragged along the floor, my heart someplace else. Shit, they were teenage girls. This was never right. What the fuck was my father playing at? I knew he was an evil bastard but kids? He'd recently started to take kids in, training them into Phantoms but I'd never been given an order to kill any. And even worse, who the hell had given the order? Which depraved fuck relished in the slaughter of a child?

Tracing the length of the wire from the alarm system, I slipped the blade from my pocket and severed the line before picking up a stone from beside the door. Smashing the small window, I reached in and twisted the key, unlocking the door. Christ! Did this family have no regards for security, especially leaving their teenage daughters home alone for the night? Someone, anyone come break in. Hmm, I couldn't help the small tilt of my lips at my own humour.

It was dark inside, the door leading into a large square kitchen that was only lit by a small ray of moonlight slipping between the blinds. I didn't bother to observe anything, there was no point, and this should be easy enough. I didn't need to be aware of available exits, or objects that may be needed in the loss of my weapons.

Moving silently through the hallway that lead off the kitchen I placed a foot on the bottom step to go up to the bedroom. A noise to a slightly open door on the left had me stilling, my eyes narrowing, my head tilting as I listened harder.

"I've told you no, Lee. I'm not doing it." Her soft female voice seemed to curl inside me; the unique pitch was soothing, even though she sounded frustrated. "She's my sister," she continued, "and even I'm not that cruel."

I walked silently over to the door and pushed it open a little more. She was sitting on a couch, bent over, painting her nails a sickly red as she held a phone to her ear. Her long black hair fell in front of her face, hiding me from her view as she slid the brush slowly up each nail, dipping it into the pot occasionally to recoat it.

She giggled into the phone. "No," she breathed, her soft whisper making me wince at how it made me feel. My brow lifted at her obvious flirting to something Lee had said to her. The sound of her laughter made me smile. She was so contrary, flirting one second, then giggling like a small child the next. I knew this girl had no idea of the effect she had over boys but she would find that seduction and teasing were two different things and would one day get her into trouble. Then again, after tonight she'd never... yeah.

"No, Mae's in bed and my parents are in France, some conference of my mother's."

I shook my head, pissed off with how her parents had left them alone at such a young age.

"No you can't!" She gasped. "I'm going to bed now." She sighed and shook her head but smiled to herself. "Goodnight, Lee."

She terminated the call and flung the phone onto the couch beside her. Her head tilted as she studied her toe decorating. "Oh, they'll do," she murmured to herself as her head lifted and she stared towards the TV.

I took a step further into the room, the thick carpet silencing my feet. I frowned when she stilled slightly but she didn't look up. Taking another step, I bit my lower lip when she reached for the phone again, obviously about to make another call.

As I reached out to plant my hand over her mouth, she flung herself round and bashed the phone into my face. I was too shocked that she had realised I was there that it didn't register she had taken off across the room at speed until she was yanking at some double doors at the rear.

I raced after her, and she pulled them open, looking over her shoulder to see where I was. Her bright blue eyes smashed into mine, the terror in them clashing with the adrenaline coursing through her. Her lips were parted, allowing for her deep panting, her chest stuttering as fright quickened her heart rate.

She turned again and disappeared through the doors, bringing us both into a large dining room, a huge mahogany table sat in the centre. A large black dresser sat on one wall, plates and glasses perched orderly on each shelf.

My eyes widened when a plate suddenly sailed across the room and smashed on the wall beside my head. "Wow." I laughed. "You are a feisty one."

"I'll scream," she shouted.

"Go for it. Then we can get your sister down here and get this over with."

Her head shook rapidly. "No. No, you leave Mae alone."

A glass shattered across my head. Her eyes widened when I growled at her. "Do that again and I will make this really difficult."

"Like it's not already?" she cried as she picked up another plate and held it above her head to launch it at me.

She moved around the table when I did, both of us sidestepping around it, our eyes on each other, our bodies ready to launch at the first opportunity.

"What do you want?" I noticed the trail of tears on her face but her courage surprised me.

"I want you. Simple really."

"W..what do you want to do?" she stuttered as we danced further around.

A small smile crept up my lips. "Well, I'm not going to rape you if that's what you think. Give me some credit."

Her mouth dropped open. "Credit?" she scoffed. "I… What?" She stared at me, unable to process anything with the fear racing through her.

"I have standards. You're just a little girl." I smiled at her.

Anger contorted her pretty face as she launched the plate at me. "I'm not a little girl!"

Fuck this! I was tired of playing.

I shot over the table after her. She finally screamed and ran to another door, pulling it frantically.

"Oh dear, is it locked?" I laughed when I grabbed her, my arms completely wrapping her up. She kicked at me, struggling in my arms as I dragged her across the room. Her head suddenly flung backwards, the back of her skull connecting with my nose. Pain exploded in every nerve ending on my face, making my eyes water and a choked grunt to force up my throat.

"Fuck!" I snarled when I clamped her down harder. "You bitch!"

"Let me go!" she cried, a deep sob wrenching from her as she writhed against me. My chest tightened. Shit, this was so wrong.

Slinging her face down on the couch, I straddled her back, bracing any moving parts as I fought for breath. "Jesus Christ, love. You're a lunatic!"

"GET OFF ME!" she screeched.

"Sshhh." I slapped my hand over her mouth. Her teeth sank into the flesh of my palm. The slap around her head was instinctive as I brought my bitten hand to my mouth, sucking on my own blood. "Fuck sake, you crazy bitch."

The heel of her foot thudded into my lower back. I turned round, wondering how the hell she had freed the lower half of her legs. This bitch was crazy. However, I was slightly in awe of her spirit and her fight.

I forced her face into the cushion with my hand on the back of her head and leant into her ear. "Will you stop! I'm seriously considering making your death as painful as possible!"

She froze, her body seizing up beneath me. My heart beat stuttered.

"What?" she whispered, her body completely lax underneath me.

"It's your time to die, love. I'm sorry."

She was silent, her whole spirit drowning in my declaration. "Why?"

I frowned. I hadn't expected that question. Sometimes kids were more intelligent than the hardest adult who would right now be begging me to let them live, not asking why I was ending their time on earth.

"I have no idea. You're just a job to me."

"How?"

What the fuck was this chick on?

"Uhh, I don't know, how would you like it?" I shook my head in bewilderment.

A small hiccup echoed from her before she tilted her head to the side and looked up at me. Her blue eyes shimmered under the pool of her tears, her lower lip trembled but she had this resolve about her, a steel spirit that was determined to keep her dignity.

"Please don't hurt Mae," she whispered. "You can do what you want to me, but please don't hurt my sister."

I stared at her, my heart threatening to break out of my chest. Her eyes locked on mine as she pleaded with me. My throat constricted, the bile in my stomach threatening to spray across her pale cheeks.

I turned her body under me until she was on her back looking up at me. "Do you know what I am?"

She shook her head, a tear that was rolling down the side of her face flinging off her face and landing on the knee of my jeans. I blinked at it, pressing my finger into it, the damp transferring onto my fingertip. "I'm a Phantom," I told her as I ran the tip of my finger along my bottom lip, tasting the salt in her despair. "I'm trained to kill. I have a contract to end your life."

Her wide eyes stared up at me, her chest heaving with my words as she tried to stop herself from crying. I had never witnessed anyone with as much resilience as this thirteen-year-old girl trapped under my weight.

"I'm afraid that whatever happens tonight, I *have* to kill you and your sister. It's my job."

"No!" She shook her head from side to side, her tears fluent. "No, please. Leave Mae. Tell whoever sent you that she was in

France with my parents. Or… or you could just say that you killed her and they'll never find out. Please! Please! She doesn't deserve this." Obviously she thought that *she* did.

I slid my thumb across her cheek, collecting her tears. She reached down and tore at her t-shirt, ripping it over her head, baring her small breasts sheathed by a simple white bra. "You can take what you want, you can…" She nodded to me, not wanting to voice her words. "Just leave Mae alone."

"Jesus Christ!" I stuttered out, yanking the throw from the back of the couch and covering her with it. "I'm not going to touch you. Not like that."

"Anything," she begged. "Anything."

Fuck!

I looked away, biting down the hatred curling inside me. An idea started to form in my head and I slowly lowered my eyes to her. Cocking my head, I studied her. She was exactly the right material; strong, feisty, brave and fucking crazy.

This would cause a shit storm back home, but something told me it could work.

Pulling in a deep breath, I narrowed my eyes on her. "I'm going to try something."

She frowned but gave me a slow nod.

I lifted my hand, then paused and lowered it. Shit! Lifting it again, I slapped it across her cheek. Her eyes widened as her skin blushed but she bit into her lip, nodding in understanding. She braced herself and turned her face to the back of the sofa. "Do it."

I slapped her again, watching how she reacted to it. After twenty she started flinching, her skin now sore and her tears stinging where her skin erupted with tiny blood vessels.

"What's your name?" I asked as I smacked her again.

"C…Connie."

"Connie, listen to me." She nodded, squeezing her eyes closed as I hit her again. "You're not breathing properly. You're tensing before I even connect with you. Your tears are making this harder. Your fear is making adrenaline, which in turn is heightening the pain."

She opened her eyes, looking at me curiously. "Breathe in and out slowly."

She fought with herself but I waited until she'd taken control, the deep heaves of her chest bating.

"Relax your body."

She scoffed at me, looking at me like I'd gone mad. I quirked a brow. She shrugged and took a deep breath, forcing her body to loosen. I smiled to myself, satisfied with her ability to take orders.

"Now," I whispered as I tilted her to face me with a finger on her sore cheek. "Stop crying."

She gulped but nodded, calming beneath me. Her compliance made me grin. She scowled at me but I shook my head, tutting at her. She relaxed again, taking another breath, her chest still stuttering slightly.

She blinked when I struck her twice, one on each cheek. The lift of her brow confirmed she had followed my instruction perfectly.

"Good." I slid off her. She blinked at me, confused as to why I suddenly relented. "You show promise."

"Promise?"

"Uh-huh." I made my way back to the door and turned. "You will become a Phantom two weeks after your fifteenth birthday, in exchange for your sister's life."

Her mouth dropped when realisation hit her, her eyes widening as her breath stuttered. "You're too young yet. However, don't think I will forget you, Connie. And don't think you can hide." I smirked at her. "And believe me when I say that no one can get you out of this. Tell anyone and our agreement is void. I will return and I will kill both you and your sister, but next time I won't be lenient."

I pulled open the door and looked back. "Do you understand me?"

She nodded slowly, shock obstructing her ability to function normally.

I winked, clicking my tongue at her. "See you soon."

I couldn't help the large grin from erupting across my face as I left the house. Suddenly, life didn't seem so bad. There was something about the kid that got to me. I had no idea what, but I was sure I would soon find out.

Out Now

FACADE
CODE

A DARK NA ROMANCE EROTICA

BY BEST SELLING AUTHORS
D.H. SIDEBOTTOM & KER DUKEY

You meet someone. You date. You fall in love. You marry.

The four simple rules of love....
Wrong! I'm married but I'd never met him before now, never dated him, never fell in love. I have no access to the memories of the most magical time of anyone's life.

My mind won't allow me to evoke the past, I can't remember those four simple stages.

I can't comprehend why I would have ever married someone like Dante. I should never have passed the first stage, although, I may have seen him through the eyes of the woman I once was, this me that lives, breathes here now, can't understand how we made it to the next stage.

I'm not sure, without memories, how I know that this voice inside me, telling me I would never have chosen him, speaks some truth, I just know. He's controlling, arrogant, callous and violent, and utterly hell bent on humiliating and degrading me – Like watching me falter, watching me struggle to comply and be the woman he married, powers him- as though he wants to break me piece by piece. Fibre by fibre. Until all that's here is the shell he created from a soul that I once owned.

Now my memories are slowly returning. And they show me a completely different side to meeting him. Our dates, falling in love. The Dante haunting me in the shadows of my mind is loving, gentle and utterly enamoured with me, nothing like the man with me now.

And this is what taunts me. My tender lover turned into a debauched, cruel sadist who is determined to consume my life, destroy my mind and murder my spirit.

I am, Star, and just like with some stars in the sky, the light you see is an echo, a façade, I am already gone

I am a no one.

Especially to him. To him I am the dark in his desires, the corrupt in his depravity.

The sin in his immorality.

Angel

BY D H SIDEBOTTOM

Olivia Thomas is in love, pure, simple soul consuming love. Nathan Carter is her other half, her light, her passion.

After three years of being together at university; three years of being joined, of a love so intense, passionate and spirited they thought their future was safe and endless but life always finds a cruel way to interfere and they soon find their relationship can't withstand destiny's intrusions and obstacles.

Two decades later destiny apologises and brings them back together by sheer chance, re-igniting their intense passion, connection and love but they soon find that twenty years of life, secrets and lies creates difficulties and struggles even their bond might struggle to endure.

When an evil from Olivia's past returns to haunt them and rip apart everything they have managed to build back up, can the lovers survive with their love and souls still intact…or their lives?

empathy

by KER DUKEY

Blake:

I am a brother
    I am a police detective
    I am a contract killer
    I don't want to love
    I don't want to feel
    I don't want … EMPATHY.

They say some people are born with decreased activity in the front central lobe causing them a deficiency in empathy. Maybe that's true about me but whether I was born this way or created in a moment of evil, empathy was something I didn't possess until her green eyes met mine in the mirror and I couldn't take her life.

I didn't want to feel, didn't want this woman in my life complicating how I lived but she was there at every turn. Sent to haunt me for my sins. Her light so bright she provoked a shadow from everyone she touched. When a job turns bad quickly altering my life forever I'm forced to feel. When nothing is making sense

I'm forced to face truths I never would recover from. When life drowns you in its cruelty you don't know which way the current will drag you or who you'll become once you re-surface.

Melody:

I was a daughter
    I was a student
    I was a victim
    Did I have his love?
    Did I make him feel?
    Did I have his empathy?
When the actions of a soulless killer forces sorrow into my veins I never dreamed the man healing my wounds would be the one to leave the worst scar. His love would scar my soul. Scars are permanent; I will never feel the relief from them. Will I learn to live with them, remember why I have them and learn never to let him close enough to inflict more? Will I eventually cover them... like tattoos coating them with new memories, new love and new starts? I didn't know these answers because the pain was too suffocating, the only thing I knew was they will always be under the surface lingering. He had scars too, from his sins. There is nothing that can cover them, they were too deep, too ugly, too dark and they marked us both forever.

Teaser from Empathy

I burst through the doors, the rain immediately beating against my skin, the cold droplets soaking me through but not cleansing the pain away.

Loneliness is suffocating me. I miss them so much I can barely breathe. There was no leads but they were releasing the bodies to us so they could be buried. My heart hurts so much. How can people survive loss like this?

The laughter of a couple running to find shelter is so deaf-ening, I want to scream at them to notice they have each other, they're happy and completely oblivious to the person dying right in front of them. I'm here, can you see me…? On the inside I'm screaming save me from the depths of this empty void but on the out my pain is clearly transparent because no way people could ignore the death of a soul happening right in front of them. Right?

A shiver rocks through my body making my whole body vi-brate. I stand there drenched, my clothes sticking to my skin, but I can't move. The beat from the downpour tap dancing over the ground is keeping me from picturing them, it's grounding me to this moment, the drops hitting the surface, bouncing off, expand-ing, swallowing, drowning everything beneath it.

"Puya?" Blake, barely visible through the torrent, calls to me.

What is he doing standing there in the rain? I can feel his intensity shift the air around us. My heart begins to beat hard, reminding me it could feel more than just the pain. He affected me in a way that confused and excited me all in the same moment.

His strides eat up the ground between us. "Why do you call me that?" I murmur, not sure if I'm dreaming him the way my mind has been in a constant fog lately. I wouldn't be shocked if I suddenly awoke in my dorm alone.

Droplets formed, pebbling over the smooth planes of his face and in his heavy soaked hair before running a path down his beautiful features, trickles clung from his dark, long eyelashes. He reached out to me, capturing my wrist, the pad of his thumb stroking over my small tattoo there. "Do you want to die?"

The laugh rippled through me. What a question. I thought I had died. I was living between the two realms. His eyes bore into mine, my laugh turned quickly into a sob, my hands trying to cover my face from his probing stare. My legs were weak, I was going to fall in a heap right in front of him, all my scars on display for him to recoil from.

Who could deal with someone grieving, losing themselves,

drowning in the current of sorrow right in front of them, getting them caught in the wake of my despair? Strong arms came around me, lifting me into a bridal hold. I couldn't look up at him. I reached my arms around his neck and burrowed my face into the crook there. I needed someone to catch my tears, wipe them away and just hold me, let me know I was still here.

I didn't query the fact he knew my dorm room as he opened it and walked us inside, going straight to my bathroom. I could hear the shower start and his heavy breathing as he manoeuvred around. His heart was thumping erratically against my chest.

The warmth from the water made me sigh as it poured over us still clothed. He lowered us in the cubicle with me on his lap to a sitting position. "I'm so lonely without them," I murmur into his neck before lifting my head to find an intensity so raw in his eyes it flayed me, stripping back the final layers and exposing my soul completely bare to him. "I needed justice for them but I'm not going to get it... so I want vengeance. But first I want to forget for just a little while." My breathing became pants. I needed to feel something else, I needed to feel connected. I couldn't keep dying alone, fading into nothing, I needed an anchor.

My eyes drop to his lips I feel his already hard cock beneath my ass. "Take me Blake, make me forget for just a little while, make me feel something more than the hollowness." This must have triggered something inside him because his lips crash against mine hard and mercifulness, his teeth nipping at my bottom lip. His hand slipped up into my hair, grasping fists falls, tipping my head back with force. His mouth claims my vulnerable throat, the build was already catching fire inside my core. He spins me so my back is against his chest, my ass sitting snug on top of his hard erection. He tugs my hair, wrenching my head to the side so he can re-claim my neck with his lips, sucking, teasing me. My hips move on their own, grinding against him to try and gain some friction to ease the ache throbbing between my legs. His hands grip my wet tee, ripping it from my body, making me gasp and exposing the lace bra covering my hard nipples.

Reaching for the buttons on my jeans, he tugs them open before I feel the warm solid presence of his body leave mine for a few seconds. He was fumbling above us. Before I could turn to see what he is doing, warm water eased from above, shelling down on us. I'm about to query him until his hand wraps around my front, pulling me hard against him once more, leaning me back and slipping the shower head into my panties.

The warm water massages in waves of continuous ripples over my sensitive lips, the intensity making me squirm. "Open yourself up for me," he groans into my ear.

I'm nervous but so turned on. I need the relief he is offering. I push at my jeans and panties so they move further down my legs, the cold air mixed with the heated temperature of the water makes me catch my breath.

He hisses when I slip my fingers down my pussy, opening myself for his eyes to devour. His growl and roughness as he tears the cup of my bra away, make my hard nipple impossibly harder, sending shock waves of adrenaline pulsing through me. I'm almost vibrating out of my skin.

Moving the shower head to my now exposed clit makes me quiver, the pressure was perfect and he held it in a way that his thumb was over the flow and his knuckle was stroking the delicate buddle of nerves. His other thumb had my nipple trapped between it and his forefinger pinching. I couldn't take it the pleasure was incredible and I lost myself to lust so powerful it took possession of my body and mind.

I writhe against him, his cock prodding against my ass and lower back. He was thick and long. My needy moans were loud and shameless, hitting and bouncing off the tiled walls creating an echo of chorused moans, my hands exploring myself as his did.

The build intensifies the flutter in my lower stomach and the pulsing inside as my inner walls grasped for relief. "Slip your fingers inside, show me how much you want me." His hungry growl rumbled into my ear.

I move my hand over his slowly then down to my opening, sinking two fingers inside myself. My walls grabbed greedily at me, the friction from everything all at once making my body cry out with an orgasm like I had never experienced before, igniting inside me, lighting every nerve in its path and leaving a tingling tremor in its wake.

The warmth of my cum coats my fingers as I ride every shudder out. The shower moved away and Blake's hand gripped my wrist, slipping my fingers free and raising my hand to his mouth, turning my head to watch in fascination as his tongue swipes out and then sucks my fingers into his mouth. The groan thundered through his body reverberating against my back, his lids fluttering closed. "You're so fucking pure and sweet." His lips collided angrily with mine, my own scent mixed with his exploding on my tongue. It was too much but not enough, all at once a contradiction in the perfect form.

D H Sidebottom's Links

Website: http://dhsidebottom.co.uk
FB page: https://www.facebook.com/DHSidebottom
Twitter: https://twitter.com/DHSidebottom

Behind closed doors;

Beta's – Vickie Leaf, Kelly Graham, Terrie Arasin, Michelle McGinty, Charlie Chisolm, Kim Sargeant, Di Scott, Rhonda Hardy, Ker Dukey.
Kinky Kittens Street team: Too many to list but each one is awesome.
Editor – Kyra Lennon http://www.kyralennon.com/
Cover created by: Ker Dukey
Cover models – Alli Theresa & Nathan Tetreault
Photographer – Christopher John https://www.facebook.com/CJCPhotography
Formatting – Champagne Formats

Printed in Great Britain
by Amazon.co.uk, Ltd.,
Marston Gate.